The First Journey

By the same author

Earth to Centauri series:
Book 1 The First Journey
Book 2 Alien Hunt
Book 3 Black Hole: Oblivion
Book 4 Civil War (Releasing in 2021)

Short story collections:
Deceptions of Tomorrow: Robots, Black Holes & Time Travel

'8 Down' from Saharanpur & Other Stories

धरती से सितारों तक:

भाग 1   प्रॉक्सिमा का रहस्य

भाग 2   एलियन हंट

भाग 3   ब्लैक होल विध्वंस

भाग 4   गृह युद्ध

'8 डाउन' सहारनपुर पैसेंजर: उपहास, रहस्य, रोमाँच और दहशत से भरी लघु कहानियाँ

 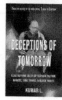

Book 1

EARTH TO CENTAURI

The First Journey

By

Kumar L.

Kumar L

Writer of Science Fiction and Fantasy

Earth to Centauri: The First Journey

Copyright © 2017 Kumar L.

First published in 2017.
This 3rd edition published in 2020 by Red Knight Books, an independent publishing firm.

Printed in India

Paperback ISBN 978-93-5419-138-1

WWW.REDKNIGHTBOOKS.COM

Cover design by Aditi Shah (aditicshah01@gmail.com)

ABOUT THE AUTHOR

Whether you want to discuss faster-than-light travel, time travel, black holes or just the latest mobile phone, Kumar is your person.

He is a tech and social media enthusiast. He enjoys travelling and is fluent in several languages. A mechanical engineer who loves pulling apart gadgets and exploring their innards, he writes science fiction stories and tries to bring future technology alive in his books.

The First Journey is the first book of the Earth to Centauri series. It is easy to read and understand and is suitable for all age groups. The First Journey and Alien Hunt, the second book in the series, are both based on themes of adventure, thrill and drama, with a positive outlook at what the future may hold for humanity. Black Hole: Oblivion is the third book in the series with the latest adventure of Captain Anara and her crew.

His books have also been translated and published in Hindi.

You can reach him on
Twitter @Captain_Anara,
Instagram @KumarLAuthor,
www.facebook.com/kumarlauthor

Visit his website www.kumarlauthor.com to learn more.

GLOSSARY

Light years: The distance that light travels in one year. It takes eight minutes for light to travel from the Sun to the Earth. Equal to about 9.46 trillion kilometres.

Faster than Light (FTL): Nothing can theoretically travel faster than light. However, all science fiction writers assume that this barrier will be broken someday and that humans will be able to reach the stars in FTL spaceships like *'Antariksh'*. Also known as relativistic speed.

Time Dilation: As an object travels at relativistic speeds, time slows down on the object when compared to a stationary observer. This is because time is relative and not absolute or fixed.

Alpha Centauri: This is the three-star solar system, which is closest to Earth at 4.2 light years. It will take us thousands of years to reach there with current rocket ships. Alpha Centauri A (Official name: Rigil Kentaurus) and Alpha Centauri B (Official name: Toliman) form a binary system, while Alpha Centauri C (Official name: Proxima Centauri) is around 0.2 light years away from AB.

Proxima B: A planet, supposed to exist in the Alpha Centauri star system circling the Proxima Centauri star. It may be suitable to support life.

Voyager 1: This was a space probe launched by the US's NASA on September 5, 1977. Part of the Voyager program to study the outermost reaches of our Solar System. Learn more here: https://voyager.jpl.nasa.gov

Golden Record: A 12-inch gold-plated copper disk engraved with sounds and images from Earth carried on board Voyager to share details of life on Earth with extra-terrestrials.
https://voyager.jpl.nasa.gov/golden-record/

Radio Telescope: A special antenna that sends and receives radio signals from space.

Electromagnetic Waves (EM): Waves in electromagnetic fields like radio, microwaves, light, etc.

Goldilocks zone: A habitable zone near a star where the temperature and other conditions are suitable for life, like the Earth.

TABLE OF CONTENTS

PROLOGUE

2087. Somewhere beyond the solar system

Its destiny was to die alone. Deep in interstellar space, with only gases and comet-forming icy particles to keep it company, it was lonesome in the black vastness.

Now, its power source was exhausted, and all instruments were powered down; it had been drifting around aimlessly for the last 70 years. Travelling at 60,000 km per hour, it had moved 60 billion kilometres through space – fulfilling its mission. No longer able to send or receive signals, it was completely cut off from its home, ready for death.

But destiny can be changed. By design, by circumstances or by sheer luck. Someone was watching it, tracking its irregular movements, checking to see if it posed a threat. This small object, with a large shiny plate covered in strange symbols, and various protrusions all along its body intrigued the finders. It was clearly artificial, but what was its purpose? Was it a weapon, a message, or simply lost in space? This object was proof that they were not alone in the universe. Perhaps there was another advanced alien civilization in their part of the galaxy.

Further investigation was merited, and they needed to prepare to meet their new friends or perhaps their new enemies.

It was taken on board and the ship turned back to where it had come from...

housed the crew quarters, communal areas, cafeteria and the *dome*. Level 3 housed the power plant, standby generators, battery banks, solar power banks, antimatter storage, utilities and escape pods. *Antariksh* could easily accommodate a hundred people, though the current number was fifty-five.

Though Faster-Than-Light or FTL speeds had been made possible by 2085, sustaining the same for extended periods of time with humans on board had required scientists to come up with path-breaking applications of quantum mechanics. Even then, managing the power requirements with a combination of fusion reactions and controlled antimatter explosions had taken almost a decade to become a reality. The tricky part had been controlling the time dilation at sub-light and faster-than-light speeds. To protect the human crew from the impact of time dilation experienced during FTL, the *dome* had been constructed to enable a mix of suspended animation and isolation from all external references. It was almost akin to a cocoon or a bubble. The ship itself was encased in a special EM field which protected the equipment at FTL and the crew at sub-light. Whenever the ship travelled at more than a few thousand kilometres an hour, it was completely isolated from the outside environment.

As they went down to the dining room, Anara could not help but feel pride in her role of commanding the first manned flight in interstellar space. This was strengthened by the fact that her country had entered the twenty-second century full of power and hope – becoming a beacon for the rest of the world. The international crew on board was a bonus. She smiled at the memory of the thousands of people who had applied to become a crewmember on the ship and how she had the privilege of handpicking every member of the crew. The weight of the responsibility for their mission sobered her up. She was responsible for the lives of fifty-four people deep into space.

Two light years travelled, two and a half more to go till they reached the Alpha Centauri star system, the farthest humankind had ever gone before. Their mission was to prove without doubt that humans were not alone in the Universe.

22 YEARS AGO, 2095
Giant Metrewave Radio Telescope, Pune

The anomalous signals had been coming through since the New Year, but most SETI listening sites had ignored them, just because they did not monitor that particular bandwidth. However, the Giant Metrewave Radio Telescope (GMRT) near the megacity of Mumbai-Pune on that particular evening had been incidentally on the correct frequency. But here again, these signals were downloaded, analysed by the algorithm which classified them as irrelevant, treated the data as routine interference and made it ready for storage.

The search for extra-terrestrial signals was more than 150 years old, and over time the study of such signals had become a mere routine, most being handled by automated algorithms or simply getting stored in vast data banks for later analysis. Despite numerous false alarms, nothing concrete had been discovered to date.

What was different this time was that the signals repeated. Once more they were downloaded, verified and catalogued. It was only when this happened a third time that the system flagged it off for human evaluation. The technician on night duty looked up from the game she was playing on her virtual screen when a red button started flashing in a corner. She reviewed the inputs, swiping across screens, but the numbers did not lie. She pushed her drink aside, forgot her high score in the game, and cleared her data pad. She needed to verify everything, but if the signals were correct, this was momentous. She settled down to many hours of work decoding the signals. Unfortunately, she was alone in the room with no one to share her excitement. Her contribution was lost to history.

It was late the following night when the guards found her running across the campus to the Director's office, alongside the head of her own department. They burst into Director Sawant's room and caught him swiping data sheets into his pad, closing up for the day. He frowned at this unannounced intrusion. Scientists, especially those in senior-grade, did not just burst into the Director's room without sufficient cause. As they rattled out their findings, a smile spread across his face. The intrusion was sufficiently justified, after all. He clapped his hand on the shoulder of the department head, shook hands with the tech and escorted them out the door, admonishing them not to discuss their findings with anyone. His stature at GMRT did not give him the opportunity to be able to jump for joy at this piece of information, and he had to be content in punching the air several times. The thought of going home was now forgotten as he sat back at his desk, called his AI for assistance, and pored over the data.

***

Four days had passed since the signal had been received and it was time to bring everything together to decide what the next step would be.

"Morning, Director," Doctor Aryan greeted. "We've completed our first cut analysis of the signal. Surprisingly, it was easy once we put together the repetitions in a sequence."

"So, what did you find?"

"It's in Morse code; dots and dashes," replied Dr Aryan with a deadpan expression while smiling inwardly. He knew exactly what would follow.

"You mean it's a rogue," sighed Director Sawant, his excitement suddenly wearing off. Rogue signals were Earth-generated signals, sometimes captured in the giant radio telescopes by accident. There had been plenty of those across the world.

"No, sir. I mean, it is Morse code, but it's definitely extra-terrestrial. Its frequency would never be caught by our telescopes if it were transmitted from Earth," stated Dr Aryan, still holding on to his flat expression.

"You don't say, Aryan! That's outstanding! And what's in the signal?"

"It's a SOS."

Sawant grew red in his face. Trust the young scientist to play a prank on him. "Are you serious, Doctor? You are telling me that we finally have a signal from outer space and it's in Morse code that went out of use over a hundred years ago? And that it signals S.O.S?" Sawant bushy eyebrows rose in unison.

"Yes, Director." Aryan's face finally broke into a smile. "I was as surprised as you are, but my team is absolutely certain about their facts. It cannot be anything else."

Sawant looked around at the eager faces surrounding him, as he digested the information, still not fully convinced. "Aryan, how's this possible? Even if some other intelligent life discovered the basic principle of Morse code, they'd certainly not use the same set of symbols, would they? This is illogical. You've made a mistake. Check again."

"There's no mistake, Director. I'm dead certain of my findings. And to quote my favourite 19th century detective: 'If you've eliminated everything else, whatever remains must be the truth.' I am forced to conclude that someone outside our solar system has sent this signal to us. They have managed to learn the simplest code that is able to travel long distance, and which can still be understood by us. The 'hows' and 'whys' are beyond me at this moment. But I believe it's not an actual call for help as the SOS suggests, but rather a signal in its simplest form telling us that someone out there in space knows about Earth and has sent back a message we can understand, as demonstration of their presence."

"Maybe someone on Earth generated a Morse code signal that travelled across space, got reflected or refracted around one of the outer planets and is being repeated by one of our satellites?" Sawant persisted with his counter argument.

"No, sir. That's not possible. The strength of a terrestrial signal would be able to travel to another planet, but it would be too weak by the time it reached even the nearest star. There is no question of it being reflected from inside our solar system, right? I'm absolutely certain; this is from some other origin." He paused, looking down at his notes, then picked up another line of thought. "I must also point out that this is a signal directed at us and not merely a general transmission that's fallen by chance in our lap. Its strength and the focused narrow-band indicate that it was specifically directed at Earth."

Sawant finally capitulated. Aryan had logical answers to all his objections. He decided to accept the fact that the signal was genuine. For now, at least. But then he had suspected as much when he had carried out the preliminary analysis. Aryan was corroborating his own findings. Nevertheless, they needed much more analysis and much more data before they could make the final determination. Many careers had been broken by unverified findings in their line of work.

"Do we know anything more about its origin?" he asked.

"After extrapolating all the data, the most likely permutation gives us an approximate distance of five light-years to the source of the transmission. That would of course mean that it's at least five years old, the minimum amount of time it'd require to travel this distance at the speed of light."

"And...?"

"That's all I have for now, sir. We're still isolating some other signals from the background noise and we're hoping to get some more clues. It's going to take some time, I'm afraid."

"Fair enough. Let's meet again tomorrow. You do realise, don't you, that if this turns out the way you are expecting it to, then it's monumental! Now, get on with it and come back with even better news, will you? And, good job!"

***

As he walked back to his room, Sawant looked up at the clear sky, riddled with twinkling stars interspersed with lights from flying vehicles. If what Aryan had surmised was true, and Sawant agreed with the conclusions, then GMRT would not be the best facility for further action. It was time to call in the Indian Space Command. He decided to immediately flag a message to the Director of Indian Space Command. In matters of such importance, GMRT usually deferred to the ISC headed by Director Srinivas.

Srinivas hung up on Sawant thanking him and added his own advice about restricting further spread of the news. He pulled out his best team of analysts and put them on the job, taking over the project and the entire signal analysis from GMRT.

The finding was classified 'Top Secret' immediately and the bureaucracy notwithstanding, the news reached the PMO within a day. In his characteristic way, the Prime Minister decided this was to be run by scientists and not civil servants. He personally put Srini in charge of the whole project and added Dr Aryan to the core team.

22 YEARS AGO, 2095
The signal decoded

The data lab at ISC was much more advanced than the one at GMRT, and at that moment there was an air of subdued excitement pervading the place. Two armed guards stood outside the door and entry was strictly regulated. In fact, in keeping with its 'top secret' status, the entire building had been evacuated.

Aryan was meeting with his team over the results from the preliminary analysis. The question in his mind was how to identify the location and distance of the source of the signal. He wondered if the answer was hidden in the data downloaded on the GMRT servers. Even though his team had the most powerful computers at their disposal, some data simply had to be interpreted by scientists.

"Dr Aryan, we've identified two new streams of repetitions in the transmissions after isolating all the random noise," Doctor Sneha said.

"And what do these streams indicate?"

"They seem to be part of some sort of coordinates, but we've been unable to get a fix."

Aryan leaned back in his chair contemplatively. "Tell me, Sneha, did you know that when we sent the first probes into space from Earth, they contained a lot of information, including the location of Earth in reference to galactic markers? So, if you were an alien intelligent civilization and your astronomy was similar to humans, what markers would you use?"

Sneha thought for a moment. "Galactic centre for one and maybe the brightest star in our side of the galaxy." she finally offered tentatively.

"Great! Let's run with this theory for a while. We take the galactic centre as a reference and assume that the signal is no more than a few years old, thus discounting for galactic shift, we get our zero-zero coordinates. Now, let's try to plot the numbers against this reference." He pushed back in his chair and stared at the ceiling for a few moments before speaking up again. "There were some references to the ancient space probes. I recall something I studied in college. Tell you what, you continue your analysis," Aryan said as he stood up, "while I go and refresh my memory. Let's meet back here in a couple of hours."

***

Aryan's first task was to call the facility's AI. Most AIs across the world, despite the physical borders, were interconnected: free exchange of information was one major achievement of the 21st century.

"Hey, Gomti. I need your help. Retrieve records related to space probes launched from Earth from the year 1950 onwards," he specified, as he poured himself a hot cup of tea.

"Doctor Aryan, one moment please." There was a short pause, and then Gomti spoke again. "A total of sixty-five interstellar probes have been sent from Earth since 1950. Fifty of them have stopped transmitting, with the last one going offline in 2065. The remaining fifteen are online and were launched between 2025 and 2050." The voice of the AI was feminine, in line with her personality.

"Hmm," the parameters of the probable search were becoming clearer to him, "run a combination check on the probes. Cross-reference information carried on them about Earth's location, if any of them carried instructions on Morse code, and those that are likely to be farthest from Earth based on their last known location."

"There are only five that fit two of these three parameters: Pioneer 10, Pioneer 11, Voyager 1, Voyager 2 and New Horizons. Of these, as expected, Pioneer 10 and Voyager 1 are the farthest away from Earth today. Contact with New Horizons was re-established 10 years ago through our radio telescope on Pluto. But I can find no correlation between the probes and Morse code."

"That's fine." A bit more progress, he thought as he drummed his fingers on the desk. "Now, I know each of the probes were equipped with scientific instruments to carry out a scientific analysis of planets, capture images and all that. But they also carried various messages from Earth, correct?"

"That's true, Doctor. Most probes carried data plates showing where they came from, including messages from Earth and mathematical formulae. Mathematics is widely assumed to be a universal language any intelligent species is expected to recognize. I can pull some data on that if you want."

"Not right now, thanks," he replied while shaking his head absently, still thinking. "Just tell me, what was the common reference point used on these probes to show the location of Earth?"

"In general, the reference points used were the galactic centre and fourteen pulsars within a relatively short distance from Earth. The information on the probes showed the distance and direction to the centre of the galaxy as well as the periods of the pulsars. I must, however, point out," continued the AI, "that the naming and identifying conventions for pulsars were not standardized when the earliest probes were launched. Further, considering various factors, such as space motion of the pulsars, it may not be possible to exactly identify all fourteen original pulsars, even by me. The information available is simply too limited."

"Okay, Gomti, got it. Can you reference the last known locations of the probes, the location of the 14 possible pulsars as well as the galactic centre and send the information to Doctor Sneha? Also, download the contact data that was on each of these probes and send it to my station. Okay?"

"Of course, Doctor."

He now knew what to do. It was becoming evident that this signal indicated intelligent life somewhere in the galaxy. He felt his face flush as the realisation hit him – this could be the greatest moment of his career! His team just found life on another planet! The two hours available to him would require complete attention to everything the AI could tell him about the probes, and he bent his head as he listened carefully, taking copious notes on his data pad.

***

"So, Sneha, have you managed to confirm the information?" Dr Aryan asked once the team had assembled back in the conference room.

"Yes, sir," she replied, nodding her head. "The direction and distance seem to indicate the origin as approximately four light years away in the general area of our nearest triple star system Alpha Centauri."

"As you will recall, Doctor," Sneha said, "this is the same place where we discovered a possible habitable planet called 'Proxima B' nearly 80 years ago. However, no evidence has since been found to validate this hypothesis. The earliest we can expect a confirmation is when the Chinese deep space probe, Yang L5, reaches it in about fifty years' time."

"That would fit in with my findings too," Aryan agreed and told them briefly what he knew about the deep space probes.

"Records from that era are sketchy, and most people who worked on the program are long dead. I did, however, find that each of those probes carried substantial records about Earth - its people, origin etc. Particularly noteworthy is the golden record on Voyager 1, which had substantial information including the spatial references that you guys worked on. We do seem to have a few answers and a rough location to go on. I think we can meet with the Director again. Gomti, ask Srini sir to meet us in the discussion room."

The meeting adjourned and three of them headed toward the conference room. It was late in the evening and the short walk to the main block was pleasant. Each of them wandered along, thinking about the implications of their discovery over the past two weeks, not knowing what it heralded for humanity.

2117
Complications

Just like most commanding officers who rise from the ranks, the captain dreaded routine admin tasks. Some of these, however, could not be delegated, and protocol required her to manage them personally. One of these was the daily roster and going through the personnel assignments.

She sighed and closed the last file on her screen. Sitting across her was Ryan, jotting down the necessary notations and changes that he had to execute. They were a good team. Over the last few years during the fit outs and trials they'd both learnt to understand and trust each other.

Ryan was ambitious, but not overly so. He knew he had a lot to learn, and with more than fifty space missions under her belt, Anara was an excellent mentor. Her ability to logically think through problems and his ability to execute to perfection made them a good fit. Sure, they argued quite often, but none of those arguments derailed the mutual respect they shared.

Anara had grown up in the foothills of the Himalayas. For her, home would always be Kasauli, a small town in the hills, still relatively untouched by technology. She had been born to a family of bureaucrats and had a good understanding of politics, both local and international. The world had changed in the last century and she had seen some of it first-hand.

The conflicts across the world early in the 21st century had fortunately been contained by a combination of diplomacy and military might by 2050 and an all-out third world war had been avoided. Relative peace reigned across the globe, but these events had led to several changes in power structures.

The expected coming together of nations did not take place and with the complete breakup of the EU in 2040, no other nation-states were willing to go through that experiment again. There were still walls across international borders and a few new ones had been built. The exchange of people became difficult, but an exchange of information flourished and that contributed to the successful launch of this mission.

Anara pulled herself out of her reverie. "Do we have anything else to cover before we go into the staff meeting?" she asked.

"No, that's it," replied Ryan, "but I hope you remembered to go through Doctor Khan's request?"

"Yeah, I skimmed through it and I have a couple of questions for him." She got up from her seat and Ryan followed her out.

They walked through the door into the staff room where the core operations team of *Antariksh* was waiting. Besides the Doctor, the team also included the engineering head, Madhavan, and the security specialist, Major Rawat. Science head, Dr Lian and Lt Manisha as propulsion and communication specialist completed the team.

"Morning everyone! This is our thirty-second week in space and 2.2 LY from Earth, and that puts us at roughly 2 LY from our destination," said Anara, pointing to the navigational display. "From now on, I expect increased focus on system readiness and weekly drills to ensure everything's in order for our final approach," she continued. "All section heads need to plan for those, alright?" Turning to Dr Khan, she asked, "Where are we on the radiation study, Doc?"

"It's all under control, Captain. I've identified ten of the crew-members from various sections who I'd like to study. I already have the baseline data of each crewmember, and Narada has compiled the changes over the last thirty-two weeks. There's no cause for concern as of now. Looks like the *dome* and the shielding on the ship are doing a good job too."

"Good. What exactly would you be looking for in these ten people?"

"This is part of the protocol that was set up before we left. This is the first manned space flight into interstellar space, and we have to study the effects of humans staying in the *dome* for extended periods of time. It basically helps us determine if there are any adverse effects on human physiology of travelling at FTL speeds. I need to run those tests more frequently and adapt the ship's shielding in case any ill-effects are found."

"Ok, yeah, I recall the briefing documents. You can handle the specifics, of course, and let me or Ryan know if you need any support. Anything else?"

"I also require space in the science lab to store some samples and carry out tests. The medical bay can only accommodate fifty percent of what we want," he stated.

"No way," retorted Dr Lian. "I've already said that I cannot allow any experiments in our science labs. Captain, you promised to work this out." Her short, petite frame made her anger a little incongruous, but she could be fierce when upset.

"I know, Lian," Anara replied soothingly, "but unfortunately there's nothing else available and this was the original plan. Moreover, your detailed work will not start till we reach our destination. I'm sure Dr Khan's 'patients' can be taken care of by then."

Lian agreed reluctantly but stared daggers at Rafiq Khan for having brought this up again.

"Now, about those power drains - any updates Madhavan?"

"Nope, ma'am," the engineer replied. "Checked most of the systems and I haven't noticed any anomalies. The thing I can't get is even though the power consumption is higher than expected, the reserves are not getting stressed. Can't explain it. I believe there's more at work than merely a system failure, but unless I get into the depth of the engines, there's very little I can do. Unfortunately, I can't achieve anything further till we come to a dead stop."

"Narada, do you have any inputs on this?" asked Anara.

There was a second's silence before Narada responded. "No, Captain. I have not detected any significant anomalies."

"There's something else needing your attention, Cap, but maybe later," Madhavan said quietly.

Madhavan's casual manner of addressing her had been annoying in the beginning, but that's just the way the engineer was. She'd chosen to ignore it. *What was so important that it couldn't be shared even with the senior officers?* Anara wondered. "We'll meet up in engineering later today, Madhavan. Right now, let's go over the communications protocols."

She had been briefed intensively on this before leaving Earth. It had been deemed necessary that the commanding officer of the mission should handle all interspecies communications, if any. Anara had been exposed to the work done over the last hundred plus years in interstellar communications.

Communications with Extra-terrestrial Intelligence, or CETI as it had been known since the late twentieth century, was a favourite among astronomers, scientists and science fiction writers. Mostly, it was deemed that two civilizations from different planets would not be able to understand each other unless a large amount of language samples and references were available. It also required sufficient time for analysis and learning. Then again, mathematics was deemed to be the universal language in the universe, and most messages were composed with this in mind.

A number of projects in the 20th and 21st century, including the Arecibo message, Lone Signal, and Contact Humanity amongst others, had attempted to send signals to star clusters in the hope that they would be captured and translated by aliens, leading to contact with Earth. Most messages were based on simple and universal understandings of mathematics and physics. Based on calculations, they would have been received at the destination before the year 2050. However, replies, if any, would still take decades to reach Earth.

Anara was carrying a standard set of greetings and basic data that had to be transmitted if contact was made. Vetted by a set of scientists, historians, astronomers and linguists, this set was determined to be the first line of making contact. Starting with the simplest form of data like ones and zeroes, increasing in level of difficulty - going up to complex mathematical equations and algorithms. It included images, sounds and videos, which Anara had learnt were similar to the Voyager golden record, though these were more voluminous.

"We have the data set ready and tested multiple times. Madhavan, what can you tell me about the transmission methods?"

"Well Cap, there are three types of signalling systems with built-in redundancies, visual, audio and electromagnetic. I'll be carrying out checks on them over the next two days but don't anticipate any issues," Madhavan replied.

"And when will you carry out trials, Madhavan?" Anara asked.

"Already underway. We've been using the given protocols and transmitting them across the three subsystems and haven't found any problems so far."

"Good. That's it then. We're set. Manisha, please plan and inform the crew about the next *Jump*. Madhavan, walk with me."

"Yes, Captain," replied Manisha as everyone stood up to go back to their respective stations.

***

"What's the trouble with the power consumption?" asked Anara as they walked out of the Ops room and down the stairway to the engine room on level 3.

"Cap, there's a systematic drain on our power resources. I've been unable to trace it to a single source. It's not a coincidence or a failure, but rather a leakage. Come. Come. I'll show you at my station."

They entered the power plant. It was a large but quiet place with most of the action happening behind shielded areas with no human access. A few portholes allowed physical viewing of the ship's engines. Drones moved in the workspaces carrying out various tasks while a multitude of monitors and displays glowed with activity, showing the status of the subsystems in the control room. Most systems had multiple redundancies, and two engineers were generally sufficient to manage this apparatus.

They moved across the hall to Madhavan's workspace. He switched on his monitor and manipulated the controls to pull up some data.

"Do you see these subsystems and the power consumption getting recorded here?" Madhavan asked, pointing to the numbers and graphs. "Those numbers add up to the overall power consumption for the ship displayed here," he pointed to another number.

"Okay," said Anara, reading the numbers, but not grasping their significance. "What exactly is the problem?"

"See here: if I take the readings from the field instruments, I find a 0.1% variance across all systems. That adds up to a total of 2% loss in power, which we can't account for," Madhavan said, showing her the data.

She finally understood what the engineer was trying to say. If this was correct, then this was a cause for worry. "Did you ask Narada to analyse these numbers?"

"No, Cap. I thought about getting him involved, but Narada is connected to every single system on board, including the field instruments. There's no way he could've missed this. But has he raised a single alarm? No! In fact, every time I have asked him to check the numbers, he insisted that the system readings are correct. That damn piece of machine." He gritted his teeth. "To tell you the truth, I've been working the old-fashioned way to avoid him," he said and showed her a stack of handwritten notes.

"If, and it's a big if right now, we assume that your data is correct, are there any theories as to where the power is being diverted?" asked Anara.

"Nope," replied Madhavan, shaking his head. "The drain seems to be hard-wired into the primary power distribution. Unless I physically open the cables, can't get to it. Opening the cables will require stopping the engines and purging the engine space of radiation. Can't do that while we are cruising, can I? And I can't hide the work from Narada."

"Don't you think you might just be overreacting where Narada is concerned? Anyway, let's keep it between us until we get a better idea of what we're dealing with. For all we know, this might just be a calibration issue. Keep your data for now and we'll confront Narada when we have more evidence."

Did the ship's AI have a system error or worse? Had it started working on its own agenda for its own reasons? Anara wondered about this as she walked out of the room.

Meanwhile, Madhavan went back to work at his station. He knew he had to find the source of the power drain soon. He was ready to stake his professional reputation that this drain was by design, but he could not figure out the reason. The plant would, of course, continue to generate enough power to take care of the drain. But that was beside the point - he still needed to get to the bottom of this mystery. Maybe he could get Manisha to help him. The kid was smart and knew everything there is to know about engineering principles. Besides, she looked at him with respect, which was damn difficult to get from young people these days.

22 YEARS AGO, 2095
Plans

The waiting area outside the PMO's cabinet briefing room was sparsely furnished. A grey carpet, a few plants, some pictures of leaders and a large flag of the country adorned the walls. The chairs were quite uncomfortable, and Director Srinivasan shifted his somewhat large frame uneasily. He had arrived quite early for his meeting with the Prime Minister and was getting fidgety having waited for the best part of an hour.

Having examined the portraits in detail, he sat down and tried to relax as he went through his notes, starting with the first time the signal had been recognized. His team had done a solid job bringing together fragmented bits and pieces to form a logical theory. The probable location of the source of the signal was quite plausible and had been confirmed by astronomers to be a possible host to harbour intelligent life. Proxima B was going to get very famous very soon. He felt prepared to answer any questions that may be posed in the meeting. The findings were historic; hundreds of years of work were culminating towards a decision. Based on all the available data, he would recommend a very ambitious project to the Prime Minister. His only regret was that he'd not be personally able to join the mission, but he had just the person in mind to lead it.

The door to the cabinet room opened and the PM's secretary ushered him in.

"Good Morning, Director Srinivas," the PM greeted, pointing him towards a chair. Srinivas recognized four people in the room.

"You know the Minister of Space Exploration and the Defence Minister. This is Dr Subramanian, Director of Defence Research and Dr Priya, Director of Institute of Astrometric," Srini acknowledged each of them in turn. This was a high-powered meeting but judging by the absence of other ministers he assumed that the PM wanted to keep the information contained for now.

"So, Srinivas," said the Prime Minister looking at him with piercing eyes, "I believe you've made progress in deciphering the mysterious signal and that you have some recommendations for us. Before you start, can you update us on the current status? These people are a bit behind and I'm afraid I'm not the best person to explain the technicalities."

"Yes, of course, Mr Prime Minister," Srini said and collected his thoughts. "Ministers and Doctors," he said formally, "you are all aware of the signal that was received at GMRT a week ago. You're also aware what the signals represent - we may finally have first contact. Let me now tell you what we have discovered since then." Srinivas swiped his forearm and connected his data feed to the conference screen bringing up his proposal. He explained how his team had extracted the second set of numbers from the signal and extrapolated the data available to locate the most probable source. The background work was needed to ensure everyone understood the base established so far.

"We believe that all the data on hand clearly indicates that the signal was artificially generated and sent from about four light years away." He swiped again bringing up a new image which he then projected on the 3D holograph. "These 7 systems are within 10 light years from us," He pointed out each with a finger, "Barnard's star, Wolf 359, Lalande, Sirius, Luyten, Ross and the nearest one Alpha Centauri. Of these, Alpha Centauri is the only system within that range. It has a binary star system Alpha Centauri A and B, and a third component star Proxima Centauri. Further there are four, possibly five planets orbiting the three stars, and one known possibly habitable planet, known as Proxima B."

"Hmm… that's interesting, of course," said Doctor Subramanian, "but back up a little. How certain are you that the signal generated outside our solar system? It's not merely some sort of, I don't know… reflection of a signal sent from Earth itself."

"Yes, sir, I'm certain," Srini replied with confidence. "That's the first thing we checked for. You see, the key reason is the lack of phase difference. Any signal transmitted from Earth and reflected back would have subtle changes in the frequency as it travelled out of the atmosphere. We did not find such a shift. What's more, if this was from one of our own satellites or the station on Pluto, there would be a record of it here on Earth and the frequency band would be different. We've not found these either. The wavelength is useful to transmit over extremely long distances – I'm talking about light years here. It was literally in the same band as cosmic white noise. No, we are dead certain about it sir, the signal is extra-terrestrial."

Dr Subramanian passed a knowing look to the PM who nodded back. Their own briefings had corroborated these findings. "Let's say we accept that the signal was sent from a distant star system using Earth codes. We can also accept that it was followed up by a second signal indicating its origin - all of this in the form of coordinates that we are able to understand. Then it would be logical to assume that these are from another intelligent civilization, which is at least as advanced as ours. These are all valid arguments on the face of it. But tell me this – how did they learn our language? Our other contact programs in the last several decades have not been successful. There have been zero responses to the signals that we have been beaming into space. What's different this time?"

"We struggled with this question too, sir," replied Srini. He had anticipated this question as well. His team had laboriously eliminated all other options. "I believe we may have a possible explanation. As you know, besides sending out signals through radio telescopes, we have been doing one more activity, and that was sending probes into space carrying sophisticated instruments and data. Our working theory is that one of our probes sent in the late 20th century may be responsible for this," Srinivas said.

He went on to explain the journey of Voyagers 1 & 2 as well as their golden records. "We've not been able to determine if Morse code was part of the messages carried by Voyager, but it's highly probable. Most of the records of that time are missing or simply insufficient. The technology of using gold plated discs itself is primitive, but it would have made the discs remarkably durable. We will try to get more details from NASA but I'm not very hopeful that they will be able to unearth more than we know already."

"I'll also see what I can do to influence NASA." The Prime Minister was a fast learner and had already moved on to the next steps. It wasn't mere coincidence that he was known for his decisiveness and ability to grasp at the core of issues. "Is the background clear?" he asked and everyone present nodded. "Then, Srini, let's hear what adventure you are proposing. There are, of course, many possible responses that we've already evaluated, but I want to hear your thoughts, anyway."

"No adventures, sir," Srini replied with a smile, "just a long voyage." Now was the chance for him and ISC to play the role of leading the world in finding a way to reach outer space. "I would like to propose three courses of action to you. First, I ask for your approval to send back a focused signal to the Centauri system, acknowledging this code. To cover our bases, we will also send similar signals to the other stars within the 10 light year distance. Second, we should open up the defence communications setup to work with GMRT on faster than light transmission. We have the ability to send signals at faster than light speeds over short distances, but most of the technology is still classified. Lastly, I recommend preparations for a manned mission to go to Alpha Centauri and establish personal contact with whoever sent the signal." He'd kept the most important item for last - anticipating what would happen next.

"Hold your horses, Srinivas!" the Defence Minister interrupted, raising his voice. "Even if we do approve all these requests, we still don't know anything about these ... these aliens! What are their intentions? How do we know they're not looking to go to war with us? Prime Minister, you mentioned it a while back and I'd like to draw your attention to our briefing on the Blue Book on aliens. Until they are deemed peaceful, we are to avoid all contact. Those people who sent out those damn probes a century ago, unknowingly or otherwise, have put us in danger today!"

"With all due respect, sir," countered Srini equally forcefully, "it is neither probable nor likely that anyone is waiting to destroy us at Centauri. One only finds alien races bent on destroying Earth and humans in science fiction movies." *Have I gone too far? I don't really care. This was science not fiction.*

"I agree with Srinivas, Minister," said Priya, coming out in his support. "We must understand that whether we're alone in the universe or not, is as much a question for other intelligent species as it is for the people of Earth. For all we know the people on Proxima B might be having a similar conversation about us right now."

"Unlike them, however," it was Subramanian who spoke up now, "we haven't received a golden record giving us information. They surely know much more about Earth than we do about them. Maybe, just maybe, there is a probe from Centauri floating toward us as we speak which will have the answers we seek, but we have not found it yet, so we must accept that we are at a disadvantage. That, however," he continued, "should not prevent us from moving forward. Anyway, the golden record clearly set out the peaceful intentions of the people of Earth and our knowledge of science. And if the aliens' intention is to go to war, why give us notice?"

"Your words mean nothing! We... have... no... proof!" the Defence Minister enunciated every word. "The possibility of a catastrophe remains, and we must be prepared. I urge you to consider a military response. If we agree to a manned mission, then it must be controlled by the military and not by civilians. We must get ready for war." His face was florid as he glowered around the table. No one had the seniority to overrule him except one.

"But... but that will accomplish nothing except maybe prompting a similar response from the aliens!" Srinivas protested. "This is a once in a lifetime opportunity. We cannot handle it with force!"

"I must agree with Srinivas, Balraj," the Minister for Space said, trying to calm things down. He stroked his chin thoughtfully, the academic in him shining through.

"Remember, humanity has always risen to the challenge of exploring the unknown and this time we have both an opportunity and a destination. Just look at the progress we've made in the last century to overcome our base instinct of making war. Let's not give in to our fears now."

This did not convince the Defence Minister. He had fought in the wars and he had lost good soldiers to enemy bullets. The terrible smell of blood on the battlefield was something he could never forget. He was also wary of the promises made by technocrats, but the faces nodding around the table told him that this was one battle he would not win. That may be true, but he was already formulating a plan to keep his beloved country, and by extension Earth itself, safe.

The Prime Minister had made his decision even before the briefing had begun. This was a defining moment. Not just for India, but for all humanity. The fact that the signal had been deciphered by an Indian facility filled him with pride. Maybe it was time to brief everyone on board on the work done on making FTL-manned flights a reality at the Indian Space Centre. The work started over 80 years ago with Chandrayaan in 2009 made the country a superpower in space, and it would now bear real fruit.

"I tend to agree, Balraj. Let's stop arguing about the domain for the moment until we know more about the threat. In the meantime, Srinivas, the three requests are conditionally approved. The response signal may be sent immediately. I will talk to the Security Council later today and update the leaders of the '8' on this development. We will need international cooperation to make this mission a success, but I guarantee you that India will lead this mission. When it comes to the technical aspects, I will allow you and the respective ministers to take the call. Please thank your team for their hard work on this project so far. You have made your country proud."

Balaraj was silent as he turned over this complication in his mind. Control of the mission must not be lost in the name of cooperation.

2117
The Jump

Manisha was looking forward to the next *Jump*. She enjoyed the time alone in her cocoon, being one with the ship and having only Narada for company. She always used the time to catch up on her reading. She was trying to get into advanced training at ISC to change tracks from technical to command and was preparing for the day when she would be able to lead the next generation of star explorers as a captain.

For most other people, the *Jump* brought on a feeling of claustrophobia in the *dome*, but for Manisha being alone in Ops was exciting. The windows provided an unobstructed view of the stars around her and she could convert any of them to a viewing screen to get more details. Narada handled most of the functions anyway and her presence was necessary only to take over in case of critical errors or unforeseen circumstances. The course had been plotted long before the ship had left for its journey and no manual inputs were required. But if necessary, she could herself pilot the ship in cruise mode.

Meanwhile, the crew had gathered in the *dome* and was entering their respective capsules. A headcount had been performed and confirmed by Narada; all present and accounted for. The lights dimmed as the capsules closed one after the other and the crew entered suspended animation. The cocoon was energized, and the *dome* entered a state of isolation. As the lights were automatically dimmed across the ship, all life-support systems went offline. Power was now only being used for four critical areas – navigation and propulsion, the *dome*, the hull and Ops. This was necessary because the *Jump* used up more energy in eight hours than what was used in a few days of cruising or travelling at sub-light speeds.

Manisha received confirmation of readiness through various green symbols across her station and confirmed the status.

"Narada," she addressed the AI, "the ship is ready for the *Jump*. Handing over controls to you for activation. Acknowledge."

"Affirm, Lieutenant," Narada said, his voice soft and soothing. "Now activating."

The ship accelerated perceptibly, and this continued for the next few minutes as it passed light speed and became invisible to any casual observer. The details of the quantum mechanics behind the *Jump* had been part of Manisha's engineering studies, but somehow, she still could not get her head around the fact that, during the *Jump*, the ship would be present at multiple even infinite locations at the same instance. That is just how quantum mechanics or the world of the smallest particles of matter worked; completely different to how we understand reality in the world that we can perceive with our five senses. Tachyonic fields - quantum fields generated by the *Jump* drive could convert the ship into imaginary mass, thus enabling it to travel faster than light. And in reality, no navigation was possible at all during this phase. Any attempt to force a course change would immediately tear the ship into pieces. The *Jump* could be performed only in a straight, clear line. A controlled stop could be performed in case of an emergency, but the ship would face extreme strain and even minor damage.

Limitations in navigation and the extreme power requirements meant that the ship could only perform FTL travel in stages. Sensors, radars and other instruments, embedded in the bow, probed ahead for millions of kilometres to identify anomalies and foreign objects. These instruments would be active throughout the Jump, but their effectiveness was limited by the stupendous speeds.

As *Antariksh* reached terminal velocity, the view outside changed for Manisha, as the observer. The space became dark as the light from nearby stars could not reach the ship. The windows engaged time-delay circuits to allow limited visibility. But the ship was now essentially flying blind.

The terminus for the *Jump* was displayed as a bright blue dot in the holo-image in the centre of the room. The ship's position relative to Earth and the destination was shown with a green facsimile of *Antariksh*. Nearby objects that could be a threat to the flight path were showing red, with their last measured velocity and position indicated alongside. Attempts to identify and classify such objects would be made by the ship's computer in the background and stored for later use, if required. Interstellar dust and minor objects would not be detected but taken care of by the front shielding.

The four-layer shield consisted of an outermost laser array, which sent out a continuous ray of high intensity beams to form a barrier thousands of miles ahead of the ship to blast away any large particles that came in the ship's path. This first-level shield prevented large objects from impacting the ship at FTL speeds as they would drill a large hole in the ship's body – immediately destroying it. The second layer was a magnetic screen to repel smaller space dust and other particles. Larger non-magnetic objects would bounce off against the secondary shield in the third layer which physically projected a few meters in front of the bow. It was meant to operate almost like a battering ram to absorb the impact and deflect foreign objects. Finally, the outermost part of the hull consisted of multi-layered composites, which could automatically regenerate if damaged. None of these defences could, however, protect the ship should it collide with a large object, and therefore the flight path was carefully plotted in advance.

Manisha stretched against her safety restraints. It was going to be a long shift. She looked at the various parameters of the ship's subsystems then activated her personal screen with a flick of her finger and started finishing a letter to her mother. Having grown up in a small town in the eastern part of India, her elevation to this position had only been possible due to her mother's determination and her own hard work.

Her father had been a bio-engineer working on the MG 1 colony on the Moon, trying to grow food crops. As a young child she had travelled with him to the Moon and marvelled at the sight of the stars unencumbered by the space debris around Earth. When he had tragically died during a routine mission, she had kept her zeal for space travel alive and aspired to go further into space than her father ever had.

Earning top position in her class at the Space Academy she had created waves in her town. Her subsequent move to the megacity of Delhi had been uneventful, but the four years at the academy had honed her and turned her grit into a passion. Her degree in Quantum Mechanical Engineering had prepared her well for her entry into the space cadet program of the ISC. At ISC, Manisha continued to excel in the exacting requirements of becoming an astronaut where she preferred the engineering and mechanics stream rather than the command stream for her major. Graduating just 3 years before the flight, she'd been selected for the first Earth mission into deep space.

She found the perfect mentor in her captain. Anara's width of experience and ability to build strong teams had attracted the best of people towards her command. The three-year training program preparing the team for *Antariksh* had been extremely exhausting. Yet, on the day of the launch, fifty-five people eagerly came on board for the challenge of entering space in a new ship. Over the last few months she had steadily built her credibility in the team, so much so that the captain had allowed her to oversee the last three *Jumps* from the control room all by herself, replacing Commander Ryan.

As she finished her letter, she marked it for inclusion in the next transmission to be sent to Earth. She ran her eyes over the numbers projecting in front of her and then dimmed the screen with a wave of her hand. The central hologram showed the steady progress of *Antariksh* against the terminus. In a couple of hours, the ship would be exiting the *Jump* and it would be time to wake up the crew. Then it would be her turn to rest. After that she planned to work with Madhavan in engineering to trace the source of the power leaks. They had not yet managed to isolate the reason for the leak, despite having checked nearly every system remotely. She was looking forward to programming a dedicated drone to carry out physical checks that would not arouse Narada's suspicions. They did not yet know that they had been looking in the wrong place.

"Lt. Manisha, all systems are normal, and we are 1.55 hours from the terminus," Narada reported.

"Yeah, I concur," she replied, suppressing a yawn. This *Jump* had taken on the same routine as the earlier ones.

"I detect one anomalous object reading, though," continued Narada. "Object marked M2575 has changed trajectory twice since we started monitoring it. The changes were extreme enough to be flagged by the navigation computer."

Manisha sat up a little straighter in her chair. In the past several weeks, this was the only time an object had been classified to pose a mild threat to the ship. They would need to track it in case it came in their path. The ship's future course may need to be plotted around it. "What do we know about it, Narada?" she asked the AI.

"Very little, I am afraid. The last full-scale reading was taken before the *Jump*. The current data points are only approximations with built-in time delay. The course change is confirmed, but I have no further information."

"Understood. I suggest we mark this as a priority for now. Ensure the scanners track it immediately once we reach the terminus."

"Noted for action, Lieutenant," confirmed Narada as Manisha watched M2575 seemingly frozen in the hologram image, but with three new readings below it, identifying changes in location and speed.

22 YEARS AGO, 2095
The new ship - *Antariksh*

The weather outside was hot and dry, the seasonal rains delayed by a few days. They would have to deploy the artificial weather system if this goes on, thought Srinivas as he sat brooding over the next steps in his project while on the way to his office. The autonomous flying car turned left outside his house and joined the line-up on the highway to ISC's main campus. The pod-cars on the highway had lined up end to end. Individual pods disconnected and moved off as they reached their respective destinations, while other new ones linked up so that the 'train' of cars kept moving. The only difference between the mass of pods comprising the train was the colour of the various pods. With the adoption of standardization, transportation pods were now a commodity, available at a low cost. Since they could essentially soar through air, there was no more need for roads. Flying pathways were still defined and controlled tightly to avoid accidents. The Director did not even own a pod like most people; he simply hailed one whenever he needed to go somewhere. As he looked upon the 'train', his thoughts drifted to the meeting with the PM the previous day.

What the Director had not stated in that meeting was that the ISC had already tested a prototype space vehicle that could reach FTL velocities. Tests carried out in secret at the outer rim of the solar system, away from prying eyes, had demonstrated the capability of the vehicle to carry loads far out into the universe. Of course, they still had to find a way of keeping the crew alive during 'The Jump' as the new FTL travel was called. As it is, a combination of quantum mechanics and FTL travel effects, including a stupendous amount of acceleration, were guaranteed to rip any bio-matter to shreds.

A few years ago, a breakthrough had been reported at the ISC transportation lab using something called a *dome*. Scientists believed that it was possible to create a cocoon within a FTL transport. This cocoon could be isolated from all external references. It would still be connected to the ship, allowing it to house a group of astronauts as the ship travelled at FTL speeds. The construction of the *dome* and validation in trials would take some time. Srini needed that time to construct the largest space faring vessel ever built. He had to expand the current technology used for small spaceships to one large enough to hold hundreds of astronauts at the same time.

This construction would require a huge team of scientists, technicians and workers. He could not even imagine the cost involved. Fortunately, he had been born in India, a country that could afford it. He would also have to start building a team of astronauts and engineers to man the vessel. He wondered if there was still a possibility that the military would take over the project.

Srinivas put the thought aside as his pod-car detached from the train and entered the ISC campus. Once the security device had scanned his car, identified the occupant and allowed entry, the car glided to a stop in front of his office.

As he went upstairs, he decided to share the news first with his team. He called up the AI and got connected to Doctor Aryan at GMRT.

"Good Morning, Doctor Aryan, how're you?"

"I'm good, Director. How was your meeting with the PM? Did you get the go-ahead?" he asked eagerly.

"Yes, we're good to go. We have authorisation to send the message. Did you have time to consider the composition of the return message?"

"Yes, I have. I've kept it simple as desired. Since they seem to understand SOS, that phrase will become our header. This will be followed by our location based on the coordinates provided in the message from Proxima B. Based on the distance the signal needs to travel, it'll take just over 4 years to reach the destination. Of course, we'll not be able to confirm that it has indeed been delivered until we get a reply back."

"Good. Let me know whenever you are ready. Thank you. I'll catch up with you soon."

The hologram image blinked off - leaving the Director to start his next task. He called up the schematics of the new ship he had named *Antariksh*. Its predecessor, *Akash* had performed very well during field trials. However, since *Akash* had been unmanned, it had been used in limited *Jump* trials with pre-programmed routes. *Akash* would first be retrofitted with a dome and humans would fly it to test its capability of travelling faster than light. These findings would help build the next generation of ships to carry human travellers into space. Srini set up a meeting. He was personally going to oversee the construction.

In the meantime, there was one more thing to be done: finding a crew for the first interstellar journey from Earth. He had every reason to be pleased with his choice of a commander for the mission; Anara. The captain had been his protégé for the last few years as she'd risen to command lunar flights. She was now part of the regular supply and study missions to Jupiter's Moons.

He placed a call to Anara, who was on a supply run to Europa station around Jupiter. She had landed on Europa a few days back and he expected that she would most likely be in the biosphere. The biosphere was relatively small when compared to the other off-Earth bases and was built on kilometres of thick ice.

It took a few minutes for the call to go through and the lag was a bit annoying. He realized that this also meant that the spaceship, once on its way to Proxima, would be out of reach and that he needed to have a solid plan for this eventuality.

Anara answered the call from the surface of Jupiter's Moon. "Hello, Director."

"Hello, Captain. How's Europa?"

"It's colder than hell, Director. Right now, it is 170 degrees below zero. The research station's coming along well. The basic instruments are already working, and we should have the colony habitat up and running by the next run. This is an interesting place, Director. As we dig deeper into the ice, we should be able to determine if life exists on this moon."

"Good, good Anara. However, there may be something much more exciting than Europa for you."

"That sounds intriguing. What would that be exactly, sir?"

"I can't explain this over the phone, Anara. The official orders are on their way. Come and meet me as soon as you're back on Earth."

"Sure, sir. Will see you soon. Anara out."

Next, Srinivas called in his personal assistant. Aman walked in from the main door and came to a stop in front of the desk.

"Aman, we're setting up a high priority mission to be executed over the next few years. I've already set a few things in motion. You'll find the entries in your log. I need you to keep an eye on Captain Anara's schedule and notify me as soon as she lands back on Earth."

It would take Anara a few days to get back. What would have once taken six years was now possible in days due to the advanced space technology. And in the future, with the advanced faster than light technology of *Akash* and *Antariksh* they were now on the threshold of leaving even these stupendous speeds behind in their quest for exploring the universe.

"Yes, sir," said Aman, making a note.

"In the meantime, you and I need to work on assembling a team of people who can travel to the Centauri star system and back."

Aman's eyes showed his surprise. During this mission humans will travel in space for the longest time ever attempted. So, the rumours going around were true – alien contact had finally been made!

"Yes, Aman. It's true," Srini said as if he was reading his thoughts. "We have received the first message from outer space, and we believe it's an intelligent civilization trying to make contact with Earth." He went on to brief Aman on the events of the last few days. "Now, we start by drawing up a configuration of people required to man the spaceship, starting with the captain."

"Yes, sir," Aman agreed and called up a screen. He drew up the standard configuration of ten manned missions used for exploration by ISC. "We are potentially looking at a twenty year plus mission."

"No, we are not," Srini interrupted with a smile. "We will be building *Antariksh*! We will build the fastest ship in history and it will take us to Centauri in one year."

"One year?"

"Yes, Aman. One year or less if we can manage. We have the opportunity to make first contact with an alien civilization and you and I are going to make it happen."

22 YEARS AGO, 2095
The new captain

Acclimatising on Earth was always unsettling for Anara. The changes in gravity, differences in day and night cycles, not to mention travelling at turbo-charged speeds, always threw her off-balance for a few days. She tightened her ponytail slightly, brushed down her day clothes and climbed up the stairs to the Director's room.

Anara saluted casually as she entered. She'd often worked with Director Srinivas and admired his ability to draw out the best in people.

"Good to see you back on Earth, Anara." said the Director, sounding genuinely pleased to see his favourite protege. Anara was younger than most other astronauts, but she was an accomplished pilot and relentless in her ambition and hard work.

"Me too, sir," she smiled as she spoke. "Been out there too long. So, what's the hurry, Director?" asked Anara as she grabbed a seat. She had been on tenterhooks throughout the journey wondering what was behind the Director's call.

"Straight to the point as usual, huh? Okay then. Tell me, what do you know about the deep space probes sent from Earth in the 20th century?"

Anara was confused. *Did the Director call her back for a history lesson?* He must have a valid reason and she decided to play along for the moment.

"Well, my history is a bit rusty but weren't a number of probes sent out to explore the solar system and beyond during that time? I seem to recall the names Voyager and Pioneer," she answered. "If I remember correctly, technological limitations of that time meant the lifespan of the probes was limited and most of them lost contact with Earth early in the 21st century. Also, the instruments on board were very primitive, but they gave us the first glimpse of far-off planets in our solar system."

"That's correct. You may also recall the messages from Earth that were embedded in these probes. Our hope was that someday some alien race would find and decipher the messages and be curious enough to reach out to us."

"Yes, sir. There was something about golden discs or plaques, wasn't there?" She was playing along, quite certain that the Director would reach the important bit in his own time.

"Correct again, Anara. What I want to tell you today is that someone did find the message, and they have reached out to us."

"What?" exclaimed Anara. She'd never have thought of this in a million years! "But Director, that is wonderful!" *How? Why? When?* A million questions crossed her mind simultaneously.

The Director went on to explain the findings at GMRT and walked her through some details, ending with a brief about the meeting with the Prime Minister.

"And that's why, Anara, I needed to meet you as soon as you came back from your current mission," he concluded with a slight smile on his face. He was sure he had more than intrigued her. The question was, would she take the bait or not? He wanted this to be a voluntary mission because of the dangers involved.

"I admit this is the last thing I expected to hear sir, but I am still not sure what you are saying. What does this have to do with me? Unless…" she trailed off.

"Yes, Anara, we've sent a signal back, but we also want to send someone from Earth to make contact with the aliens."

"That means you are setting up a deep space mission and you want me to be a part of the team. That is unexpected." This was huge!

"It's more than that, Anara. I want you to lead the mission. You see, since our labs have discovered the signals, it has been decided that India will host the mission and I can't think of anyone else who has the experience necessary to pull this off. Like you."

"Well, I am flattered, and I certainly hope I don't let you down," replied Anara and with that the deal was sealed. She was going to be among the first humans to cross the boundaries of the solar system!

"I'm sure you will not, Anara. We have quite a few years in front of us and I wanted someone who can be onboard from the inception. So, shall we move on to actual preparations? This will take some time."

"I'm all ears, sir," she said as she leaned forward and put her hands on the table between them.

"You have of course trained on *Akash?*" started Srini, getting up from his seat and turning around to look out the window.

"Yes, sir. Two trips to Neptune and beyond, but at sub-light speed only. *Akash* is considerably faster than anything else we are flying now."

"That's true. Only now, we have another ship on the drawing board, *Antariksh*, which is even faster than *Akash*. You will see the schematics soon enough and, more importantly, as captain you will get to choose your crew. Now, I want you to go back to your office, look at the plans and come back to me with your recommendations. Keep in mind – this is an Indian mission, but the Prime Minister has requested an international crew." His voice grew graver. "Like I said it will be many years before you actually take off. You will continue with your current work and this will, for the time being, be your side project, you know, learning about the ship, building your team, intensive long-term training. You understand?"

Anara thought it over. This was a commitment for a lifetime, not just for her career but even her personal choices. Of course, she was ready. She nodded.

"Now Anara," Srinivas continued speaking, "I can't put more emphasis on the importance of this mission and what it entails for humanity. For more than a century we've been trying to get in contact with aliens. SETI / CETI and numerous other programs have been the foundation of the success that we see today. There's been enough speculation about the nature of the alien beings that we will encounter. Unfortunately, most of them seem to end in domination or even annihilation of Earth."

"Yes, I've read about those, Director," Anara said amused, "but what I'm really intrigued with is the fact that we seem to have found a civilization so close to Earth."

"That still remains to be seen and indeed you and your crew will be the first to determine that. ISC believes that it is unlikely that we'll find a civilization large and advanced enough to mount an interplanetary war. It is more likely that our protagonists are reaching out to us with hope rather than fear or aggression."

"Your job is going to be two-fold. First, you must guide the spaceship mission through the light years between the two planets and for this the best team you can assemble will support you. Then you will be representing humanity in front of an alien civilization all by yourself. Nothing we can do can help prepare you for that meeting. That's an enormous responsibility."

Anara nodded her understanding. It would be tough. She was a good pilot and a decent captain, but she had never even remotely considered herself to be ambassador material for a whole planet.

"We could send a diplomat with you, of course, but the situation may demand fast thinking and action. This will largely remain a scientific and exploratory mission. This contact can always be followed up with more formal relations. I believe you'll be the ideal person for this purpose. You've run plenty of missions involving tough situations. You also have the presence of mind required to handle difficult people. Our hopes rest on you."

This was one of the longest speeches Anara had heard from the Director. The importance of the mission was clearly evident.

"I understand the responsibility, Director. I'll do my best," she repeated.

"Good, then you better get to work. Aman will be assisting you on this. Goodbye and best of luck. See you back here soon."

***

As Anara left the Director's office, her mind was already grappling with the planning she had to do. She had enough time on hand if the ship was still on the drawing board. She decided to start off by finding people for her crew, starting with a large pool of possible astronauts and engineers and fine tuning it over a period of extended training and fit-outs.

By the time she reached her own workspace, the AI had already downloaded the layout and other details of

Antariksh. She set it up on the holo display and tried to familiarize herself with the system. The massive ship, significantly more advanced than any she had flown till then, rotated slowly on the top of her desk. It would be like a small city, she decided, almost self-contained, after all the mission required them to spend a minimum of two years in space, probably more if things went amiss. They would be all alone, and even in case of a catastrophe, no one would be able to come to their aid. This ship could be their grave for all eternity.

Dismissing her sentimental thoughts, she switched off the display and called Aman over to help her. She was sure she would get a basic understanding of the new design in a couple of weeks, even though the science would certainly take much longer to understand.

She and Aman started composing a message to send out - asking for volunteers for a classified mission. The applicants would need to be informed about some parts of the truth and Aman would have to prepare credible stories. She also knew whom she wanted as her second in command: Commander Ryan. He had worked with her on several missions and she admired his strength of character and scientific ability. He was a perfect bulwark – impulsive when she was cautious. He would be a perfect bridge with her crew. She was an inspiring leader, but she needed someone to 'dot the i's' and Ryan was the logical choice. He was a stickler for details, wrestling problems to the ground with a blend of logic and science. A little young, like her, but they would have sufficient time to get more command experience over the next decade or so.

As for the rest of her crew, she would need a few specialists, including doctors, scientists, engineers and navigators cum pilots. Even with advanced AIs in use across the world, there were some things that a bundle of algorithms just could not be relied on to solve.

She also needed to get in touch with Doctor Aryan and his team to get a better understanding of the details of the contact signals. That would be required when she came face to face with the aliens.

With this in mind, she and Aman sat down to draw up the plans in detail and to set up the meetings and networks. The next several years would be tough, but she could hardly wait to get started.

2117
Anomalies

The indicators on the master control panels were glowing orange indicating the drains in the energy reserves were now a high priority item on *Antariksh*. While still not critical, if not addressed the steady reduction would soon be a cause for concern. Despite intense efforts, Madhavan had not been able to come to any conclusion so far.

Ryan was frowning as he went down to the power plant to talk to Madhavan and Manisha, mulling over their options. They had tried using drones and robots to open up conduits and cables but had not found anything. Short of actually stopping the ship and ripping connections apart, he did not see any way out. Anara had shared Madhavan's reservation about Narada with him and the fact that she was contemplating directly confronting the AI. Narada's recalcitrance in sharing information on this issue was worrying him too.

As he climbed down the stairs, his mind went back to when the ship was being built. He could not help but be grateful for the opportunity that had been given him. He was the first American to have reached interstellar space. Even though America had put the first men on the Moon, the 21st century had brought challenges that had taken time to resolve in terms of economy and conflict. His mother and father had both been in the US Marine corps. Their absence from home on duty tours had affected him and his grades had dropped in the early years. But his mother's discipline had helped reform young Ryan from his wayward ways. He'd managed to stay in school and get his diploma.

At the base in Diego Garcia with his parents, he'd started working very hard and decided to aim for a degree in engineering at one of the top schools. His job at the USAF had helped him complete his doctorate in Physics and earned him a secondment to NASA. He had worked on military strategy, aeronautical design and served in the front lines in the South American wars. He'd applied for this mission though NASA and with a lot of hard work and a bit of luck he had been selected as second-in-command. It didn't hurt his chances that ISC was looking for an international crew and his knowledge of propulsion systems and space quantum mechanics were required to complement the engineering team on the flight.

"Madhavan. Talk to me. Where do we stand?" he asked the engineer on entering the plant.

"Nothing concrete, sir," Madhavan replied, wiping his hand across his face and lightly pressing his temples. "The drones have done their work and we've checked every circuit we could open. No better off than when we started, boss."

"Except...?" prompted Manisha.

"Except that, while studying the drawings, we have found a small anomaly in the ship's design that we can't explain."

"One more mystery for us, is it?" Ryan was intrigued.

"Well, not so much a mystery as a flaw that could be related to our search. See here, while looking over the design schematics we've found a difference of one meter at three sections on each side of the ship. I can't account for those even if I consider all the shields and bulkheads." He thrust the design schematics at Ryan as if expecting the commander to offer him an immediate solution to the dilemma.

Ryan waved them off and stood over the table, legs apart, his eyes carefully scrutinising the various data pads strewn over it, but he could not offer any explanation. "Quite strange. Weren't you involved from the beginning in the construction of *Antariksh*? Wouldn't you have noticed any differences then?" asked Ryan.

"Not really, boss. I only started working on the program a few years after the start of construction. I'd started off as head of projects for the propulsion subsystem. I only took over as a chief in the last two years, and at that stage the hull was completed, and we'd moved on to the interior design and preparing for field trials. Manisha came in even later in the final stages, after her training in flight control and navigation. So, you see, I never actually got exposure to the hull design, except after completion of construction."

Ryan nodded. "I think it's time we brief the captain on what you've found. We must decide what to do next."

***

Anara's room was appreciably larger than that of the other crew members but not by much. It still felt cramped as the four of them sat around on two chairs, the single seater and Manisha on the small bed. Anara had enabled her privacy function to lock out the AI to avoid any eavesdropping.

Ryan briefed Anara on the situation, with interjections by Madhavan and Manisha. She listened carefully, asking some questions from time to time. When he'd finished, she leaned back in her chair, thinking about the two issues in front of her.

"Based on what you tell me, it's clear these are related," she said. "We are losing power and we have an unexplained possibly hidden compartment on our ship. It is a leap of faith, but I would wager that somehow power is being diverted to the compartments for a reason we cannot fathom right now. Let's see if more direct action will shed some light on this."

"Narada," she addressed the AI, "come online."

"Yes, Captain," Narada replied after a brief pause.

"Narada, we spoke about the power drain. We've been unable to locate the source or the area where the power is being fed. What can you tell me about it?"

"I'm sorry, Captain, my readings do not indicate any drain."

"Then how do you explain the readings from the field instruments and those gathered by the drones?" Anara persisted.

"That may be the result of a calibration error, Captain," he replied.

"There is no calibration error and you know that very well, Narada. I have personally checked the settings!" Madhavan said, nearly getting out of his seat. "You are implying that I am incompetent or maybe lying?"

"I am not implying anything of the sort. Humans are prone to errors and this can be merely one of them."

"You – you–" spluttered Madhavan; furious and unable to even complete his sentence. Manisha looked up at him, alarmed. She had never seen him this angry before.

"Easy, Madhavan," Ryan said, trying to calm him down.

"Easy my foot! This lying piece of artificial intelligence thinks it is better than humans!" Then, remembering who was in the room, he sheepishly apologized. "Sorry, ma'am!"

Dismissing his outburst, Anara turned her attention back to the AI. "Narada, that statement was uncalled for. Now, I ask you again, what can you tell me about the power situation and about the extra space in the hull?"

"I'm sorry, Captain, there is nothing in my logs to verify either of the two submissions."

With the AI steadfastly refusing to acknowledge the problem despite the evidence, not much could be done. Anara dismissed him. Direct action had achieved nothing with Narada. He was completely in denial.

"This is not going to work," she said, addressing her team. "Let's plan a shutdown after our next *Jump* and get to the bottom of this. Commander, I expect a full plan by the time we are ready to enter he *Jump*. Use whatever resources are required. This is obviously not just about the drain anymore. With Narada refusing to cooperate, we can't continue if the ship is compromised in any way. The lives of fifty-five people depend on it." Ryan nodded and made a note.

"Tell me, Madhavan," asked Anara, turning to face him. "Do you think we can fix the issue with Narada if we restart his program?"

"Been thinking about it, Cap. Narada has a failsafe built in. He can be turned off in case of extreme emergency but even then, the program only goes dormant in the central computer core. I have not found any means of completely disabling or starting him from scratch. We would also be left without a functioning AI as the backup is rudimentary. We should be able to manage a few *Jumps*, but I would hesitate to utilise the backup for our journey forward or back. Strongly recommend against this action till we are back on Earth with the specialists who constructed him."

"What happens if we do shut him down and then reboot?"

"Again, technically that is possible if we use your codes, but the core programming would still be in place when we boot up and Narada would be right back where we started. It is equally likely that we will lose all the information and activities he has undertaken since our launch and even before that. And before you ask, ma'am, no, I cannot make changes to Narada's program or troubleshoot it. I doubt anyone on this ship can. It has millions of lines of very sophisticated code. Also, messing around with AI programs is strictly regulated." Inwardly he wished he could twist the codes enough to give the AI a nasty headache.

"I know, Madhavan, but out here in space we have a bit of leeway that we can exercise if necessary. Though, I guess it won't be of much use if you can't do anything."

"Sorry," mumbled Madhavan. *Maybe I will get my wish after all.*

"Alright, so we're back to square one. We need to keep looking for options."

"Understood. There is, however, one more thing. Manisha?" said Ryan, gesturing to the Lieutenant.

"Yes, sir. This is about object M2575, which we detected a few days back. It came on our radar after two course changes not consistent with the movement of celestial bodies or other objects we have encountered so far."

"What do we know about it?"

"We've been unable to get any fixed readings as it is still too far away. It consists of metals and alloys. A spectroscopy analysis hasn't shown anything remarkable. We are still busy tracking it," said Manisha.

"Captain, M2575 has changed positions and vectors three more times since we've started tracking it. It's roughly in our path and there is enough reason to believe that it is both artificial and under its own propulsion," Ryan replied.

"You mean it could be a ship or a probe? When will we know more about this object?"

"I'm keeping an eye on it. I believe resolution will improve after our next *Jump*," Manisha confirmed.

Anara removed a stray lock of hair from her forehead. "So, we now have three anomalies to investigate. Let's split resources and get Rawat in on this as well. Manisha and I will focus on M2575, while Ryan, Madhavan and Rawat will focus on the power issue. Those are the priorities. Dismissed."

As her team left her quarters one by one, Anara composed an encrypted message to the Director of ISC and sent it through the backup transmitter, bypassing normal protocols. She did not want Narada to read her messages because she didn't trust him at the moment. Should the situation deteriorate further, someone on Earth would be aware of the reasons even if it took months for the message to reach home.

2117

3.2 LY - Contact

The alarms were blaring across the ship loudly enough to wake up the dead while the red lights cast rotating shadows piercing the darkness. In the *dome*, lights came on and disoriented crew-members were staggering out of their capsules. Anara and Ryan were the first out of the door, racing to the control station, both believing the ship had crashed into some object during the *Jump*. They'd entered stasis just a few hours back and were confident *Antariksh* could not have completed more than half the distance to the terminus. So, this had to be an accident.

Manisha was at the control station, frantically trying to acknowledge and manage the various alarms around her. She looked up and was relieved to see the Captain and Commander entering the room.

"What happened, Manisha?" Anara yelled as she ran to her station and called up various displays. Ryan moved to his own station and started barking off orders to teams across the ship. After the initial confusion, the crew was back in action and responding well as their training was kicking in. Their stations were manned and secured, the teams waiting for further instructions.

"We encountered an object in our direct flight path, Captain and the ship went to an emergency full stop. We have zero velocity and are holding position 3.2 LY from Earth," Manisha replied.

"Narada, bring up the obstacle on holograph," Anara instructed the AI as the clamour of the alarms continued in the background and red lights flashed around the room. "Someone, please turn off the damn alarms!"

The room suddenly became silent as Manisha turned off the alarms, but the lights kept on flashing.

As the holograph image stabilized, Anara got up from her seat and went closer to the holo, intrigued by what she could see. "Enlarge the image, Narada. What information do we have, Manisha?" she asked, while a steady stream of data flowed on her screen.

"The object is approximately fifty meters in length composed of metals and unknown composites. It's..." her voice trailed off as the holo became clearer, "it's a spaceship," she finally managed to finish.

The ship was a million kilometres in front of them. Its shape was strange - unlike anything the crew had ever seen before, a bulbous middle with various appendages and protrusions along every side. Even here in deep space the entire structure glowed as if lit by an inner light and the effect was mesmerizing. For the moment it seemed to be holding position.

"Captain, *Antariksh's* autopilot has responded as programmed and stopped the ship mid-flight. This has strained the major systems, but they are now coming back to full power," reported Ryan.

"Noted, Ryan. Narada, where the hell did this come from? Why didn't we detect it sooner?"

"I have checked all logs and data, and this is likely to be the object we were tracking - M2575. The radar readings are being collated, but it seems it suddenly changed course in the last hour and has moved to deliberately intercept us."

"Is there a chance that it is of Earth origin?"

"That doesn't seem likely, Captain. I have never seen this configuration before," answered Ryan.

"Manisha, get Madhavan and Rawat here on the double. I want them to look at it. Call Lian too. We may need her. Hold your position till we can determine what this thing is. Ryan, start scanning using all systems. Narada, plot a course at sub-light to M2575. Keep the course keyed in if we decide to move forward." The name M2575 was unwieldy but would have to do until they could determine the nature of the alien ship or object, whatever it was.

The rest of her team entered the room one by one to find a large holographic 3D image being displayed in the middle of the room and the data captured from the scanners floating alongside it. Multiple analysis started off on different stations.

"I can't identify the material of construction. In fact, except for the shape, I am unable to get any other details. It's too far away for our scanners to be effective and there seems to be some sort of absorbance or reflective field in place. It's preventing our beams from penetrating the hull," reported Ryan.

"Concur, boss," added Madhavan. "I've never seen this design ever before, not even in the concept stage." The rest of the crew added their agreements to his statement.

"I suggest we bring our security protocols online. This is an unknown situation and we may need to act swiftly," Rawat said.

"I agree, Major. Activate the protocols and get the security teams on standby." The ship was carrying six members of the army, all trained to provide security to the ship and the crew plus the laser weapons.

Major Rawat sent off a message to his security team and came to Anara.

"Something else you have in mind?" she asked.

"Yes. We need to get the weapons online as well. The protocols are very clear on this point."

"You'd better do it, Major."

Rawat went off to activate the four laser cannons, two each mounted on the bow and stern of the ship. Similar to the shield lasers, their power output was larger, but they were designed to track and engage at a shorter range. The power banks were charged, and each placed at his personal command. They were not yet released from their mounts. The four weapons were mostly for show since the lasers had a limited capability. He had something else planned, but he thought this was not the time to show his full hand, even to the captain. The Defence Minister had been emphatic on this point.

A couple of hours passed while neither ship made any movement. Anara wondered about her options. Her briefing on Earth had mostly concentrated on what had to be done once they reached the destination. There were no plans on what she should do if intercepted mid-way by an alien ship.

Data continued to flow across the screens, but it was now getting repetitious, as the instruments had not gained any new information. Spectroscopic analysis seemed to reveal a few new elements, but there was nothing to compare the readings with.

"Commander, I'm open to suggestions."

"I think we can close the gap. Going closer may give us more information about the ship," said Ryan.

"If they wanted us to come closer, wouldn't they have given us some indication, Ryan? I'm assuming they've been aware of our approach for quite some time and since they've reached out to us, it may be prudent to adopt a wait and watch attitude," replied Anara.

"I don't agree. I say we go ahead. We need to show that we're not afraid. We must be aggressive," asserted Rawat.

"Major, I hear you, but I'm not going to be the person responsible for the first interstellar war if we miscalculate. We have time on our side. We'll wait. I'm going to let them make the first move."

The major nodded his acquiescence while inwardly being relieved that he had not revealed everything to the captain. Didn't she understand that negotiations were carried out from a position of strength? He was a soldier and his priority would be to defend the people he was responsible for.

"I want to set up non-stop monitoring in the control station with either me or Commander Ryan constantly present. The rest of you will also break into shifts. Manisha, you and Madhavan will continue to scan the ship and gather whatever information you can."

The team settled down for a possible long haul, as neither ship had made any moves since their first contact.

***

A few more hours later, leaving Commander Ryan in the hot seat, Anara walked off to the cafeteria. She picked up a tray, loaded a few items, added a cup of hot tea and selected a seat near a porthole, away from the rest of the people. Her habit of having tea even with lunch and dinner was a constant source of amusement to Ryan. As she gazed out of the ship towards the alien object, she remained worried about what the major had said. If indeed the status quo deteriorated, all she had were four measly laser cannons. They might as well be throwing peanuts at the ship in front of them for all the good the laser cannons would achieve.

She still believed that any alien culture trying to make interstellar contact would be largely peaceful but looking back at the history of her own planet she knew bigotry was not dead. Fear would play a big role in what was to come. She wanted to talk to someone to share her misgivings and build up her confidence, but her mentor was light years away. She'd chosen to be a commander on a deep space mission, but at this moment she felt extremely lonely.

"May I join you, Captain?" Rafiq Khan interrupted her train of thoughts.

"Of course, Doc. What's on your mind?" she said as she listless put a couple of bites into her mouth.

"This may not be the best time to bring this up. I hope things are under control?"

"There's been no change, Rafiq." She knew the physician was many years her senior, but he did not mind her using his first name. He, on the other hand, remained mostly formal.

"Oh, okay. Then this is as good a time as any other. I wanted to brief you on the radiation tests, Captain. The first results on the test subjects are in. Alarmingly, the exposure readings have been rising steadily since we left the dock. They're still under the threshold and we should be safe for a few more weeks. But I'm worried that the radiation shields are not being as effective as designed."

"Go on," she said, considering his words. This was not coming at a good time. She needed to focus on the aliens, but her own ship seemed to be determined to let her down.

"You see these graphs," said Khan, as he gestured for a small screen and showed her the numbers for the crew-members under his study. "This column shows the baseline readings we took before we started from Earth. Technically, based on the many years of data we have collected and the hundreds of astronauts who travelled across the solar system, these readings should not have changed by more than five percentage points. But now I see changes five times that."

"Did you check for the type and source of the radiation?"

"That's another thing, Captain. I don't think this is normal galactic background or solar radiation. My instruments show that there is particle radiation that consists of gamma, alpha and neutrons. That shouldn't be possible, unless we're close to a strong radioactive source."

"Do you think we have a leak in our power plant? I trust that you've checked with Madhavan?"

"No. It's not from the power plant. Madhavan has confirmed that. I've used detectors and found radiation throughout the ship. It's not localised in any given area, but there must be a source. I've been unable to find it so far." He was worried, and it showed in his face.

"Are my people in any danger?" That was her biggest concern.

"Like I said, we're still quite far away from dangerous exposure levels. In fact, the radiation level is extremely low – just above detection limits. I'm just worried that it is present at all. I'm sure that it will not result in fatal exposure anytime. I don't believe we missed any critical elements in our deep space studies, but there's always that small chance. With your permission, I'd like to send the readings back to Earth and extend my studies to more crew members."

"Okay, I'll approve the request. Keep Ryan informed so that he can schedule the crew roster and keep him briefed about your findings too. You know, Doc, this adds a fourth element to our set of mysteries on the ship."

After the doctor left, Anara sighed inwardly. A few hours back she was peacefully asleep in her capsule and now she had multiple problems to deal with. She straightened her back and decided to focus on the most pressing problem at hand: what should be her next step to contact the alien ship?

21 YEARS AGO, 2096
Building the team

Anara and Aman had been poring over the hundreds of applications they'd received from astronauts and technical experts wanting to be part of the deep space flight. The announcement of India's proposal to send a manned mission to interstellar space had been greeted with enthusiasm. However, as decided by the '8', the actual nature of the mission had been placed under wraps until the vessel was ready for launch.

Anara had continued to press for Ryan to be her second-in-command and with the support of Director Srinivas, the PM had agreed to get Ryan transferred to ISC. He was finally on his way to join the mission. His wife and daughter would be staying in India for the duration of the mission where Joan would be working in the signals and communications division of ISC.

Next on Anara's wish list of the command crew were a chief engineer, a medical doctor, and a chief scientist, among others. She had been informed that Major Rawat would be joining them as a security specialist along with his team of elite soldiers. They were currently in training in a separate facility under the defence ministry. It had been planned that the security team would be independent and would only work nominally under the captain. Anara had been furious when she heard this and had threatened to withdraw from the whole exercise. She had been clear: the ship and everyone on it were her responsibility and, without exception, had to be under her direct authority. It had taken intense lobbying to the PM by the Minister for Space Exploration and Director Srinivas to convince him and the Defence Minister. The military had eventually, albeit reluctantly, agreed to the proposal.

Several junior positions were being filled with members of her old team at ISC and VSSC. Other engineering firms had come on board with their technical personnel as well. No one was going to miss a chance to be a part in this mission.

The Director's recommendation for medicine was Dr Rafiq Khan, who was a leading authority in space medicine. Having done his post-graduation from AIIMS with many years of clinical practice, Dr Khan had then spent five years on the lunar colony and another two on space missions to Jupiter's moons. His references were solid and, more importantly, his research on deep space effects on human physiology was now the standard text in medical school books. Convincing the doctor to join the mission was easy but getting him to move from research back to practicing active medicine could only be managed by Srini himself. He'd told the doctor that he'd be doing minimum treatments. Most of the medical procedures would be managed robotically and skeleton supplementary nursing support would be on hand. A chance to study effects on human physiology in deep space had finally convinced Dr Khan.

With the doctor on board, finding a head for the science team was next. Unfortunately, it would be difficult to find a single person who could fit the bill. Space exploration would require multiple skills: those of an astrophysicist, astronomer, astrobiologist, exobiologist, planetary scientist, and a geologist among others. After an extensive search, Anara had decided to have a rethink as she could not carry too many specialists. She decided to get a scientist in nominal command with a whole research team supporting her. The number of people was fixed at four - three scientists and an astronomer.

Dr Lian was the nominee from China to head this team. A planetary scientist herself, she had exposure to the rest of the sciences and was respected in the research world. However, she had never been to space beyond Mars and her orientation and training would be Anara's responsibility.

Though she had still not found an engineering chief, the rest of her team was taking shape and Anara could now devote some time to plan for the logistics of the two years they planned to spend in space. Since resupply would be out of the question, they needed a drop off and supply point. A drone ship with logistics would be sent out in front of *Antariksh* to set up supplies. *Antariksh* would interface with it at the outer rim of the solar system. The process would repeat itself on the return journey.

Reclaiming water and oxygen from all processes and by-products was the key to avoid carrying large amounts of basic requirements in space. Over many years of spaceflight humans had mastered the art of recycling almost every single drop of water and oxygen used in space. Recovery of moisture from air, human waste etc. would be the norm. Water would also be recovered from the fuel cells. Anara would be leaving this to the ship designers, and she was not too worried about this issue.

Taking fresh food would not be possible - even in limited quantities, but a mix of concentrates, pellets, dehydrated and cryogenically frozen food would suffice. Printed food from a base stock of proteins, carbohydrates, fats was provided for but had to be kept to a minimum to preserve energy. Limited cooking could be done on the ship. Medical supplies would be important, and she was waiting for Dr Khan to come on board to verify the supplies and equipment. A separate medical bay was part of the design.

Anara would be reviewing the ship's weight and propulsion data along with design engineers. Every aspect of the launch and the journey would be pre-planned, as they could not expect any support from mission control in deep space.

There was progress but much more needed to be accomplished before they were airborne.

20 YEARS AGO, 2097
VSSC Thiruvananthapuram

Anara entered the assembly area at the Vikram Sarabhai Space Centre in South India. This premier space vehicle development centre had been at the forefront of India's space exploration effort for a hundred and fifty years. Starting with the first launch of RH-75 rocket to building the reusable launch shuttle *Ganga* in 2034, it had many firsts under its belt, and this was where *Antariksh* was being built. VSSC was under direct authority of ISC, but being more involved in research and development, it enjoyed a larger amount of autonomy.

A secluded assembly area had been set up for the deep space program. Approach and access were restricted and the Director of VSSC, Dr Pratyush, led the latest program.

He met Anara at the entrance, and they walked to his office. Along the way, he explained the various activities being carried out in the cavernous area. Anara was amazed about the amount of work underway. Drones, robots and humans shared the massive workspace and there was a certain harmony during the manufacturing process she could only marvel at. She could make out the various parts of the space vessel taking shape. Pratyush told her that the engines and power plant were being built at the second VSSC facility near Bangalore.

As they entered his office, she noticed numerous technicians working at their stations. Pratyush guided her to a chair and sat down behind his desk. Several screens showed the various stages of the project while the large display in front of him showed the readiness of the vessel. There was a countdown clock adorning the wall indicating time to launch.

"I'm very glad to have you back here, Captain," he said, looking genuinely pleased. "I assume you're ready to move to T'puram with your team? The training facility is complete and so are the quarters for your crew and support teams."

"Thanks, Doctor. My team is still busy getting organised, but the key members will be joining us today. I came up a little earlier to brief you about them." She explained some choices she'd made while selecting her team. Ryan and Lian would be joining her later that day, while she had finally managed to find a suitable chief engineer.

Madhavan had been introduced to her by Srinivasan. She had immediately taken a liking to the short, slightly balding person with multiple degrees in engineering under his belt. More importantly he had ship-building experience and had been a team leader on the *Akash* project. Anara liked his absent-minded casual attitude which reinforced a brilliant mind. Madhavan was not a natural leader, preferring engines to people and could be rough-edged at times, but he was humble and ready to listen and learn. I don't need everyone on my team to be a leader, I need good execution-oriented people as well - that is what had convinced Anara about Madhavan.

Anara and Pratyush reviewed the progress of work while they waited. Soon enough Ryan, Madhavan and Dr Lian joined them. They immediately got down to business.

"I trust you have been able to go through the basic designs I sent you?" asked Dr Pratyush.

They all nodded in agreement. Over the last few weeks they'd managed to get enough time to discuss the details of the spaceship design and had come prepared. Unlike many scientists, Dr Pratyush enjoyed being an administrator, and he revelled in explaining the intricacies of the centre.

"We've gone through the schematics, Doc," replied Anara. "Madhavan has also been able to clear some things we were worried about. Perhaps we can go to the floor and see the actual construction?"

"Of course, of course! After all, it's your ship!" the Doctor said with a hearty laugh as he stood up and guided them out of the office.

They all marvelled at the feat of engineering, which was taking shape on the assembly floor. The ship was massive as could be seen from the superstructure that was almost complete. Dr Pratyush explained the various sections of the ship and Madhavan added some details that he was particularly excited about.

"It has three different levels," explained Dr Pratyush. "The top is the command level; the second level is the habitat and the bottom level is where the power and secondary systems will be. We have a central corridor on each level with two parallel escape paths along the hull. Cross corridors provide access to the rest of the areas."

"Where are the crew quarters, Doc?" asked Ryan.

Dr Pratyush gestured at a display and pulled up a schematic of the ship. "Look at level 2 here," he indicated with a finger. "Right here. We have various cabin sizes as well as dormitory arrangement. The *dome* is placed in the centre. Since the crew would spend a lot of time hibernating here in one place, we've tried to place it centrally for protection."

"These quarters look larger than the ship that took me to Mars on my first flight!" quipped Anara drawing a chuckle from the Doctor.

"Technology has come a long way in the last few years and this is the largest ship ever built. We'll, of course, be completing the final assembly on the Moon, which will allow work to proceed faster and take-off will be easier," stated the Doctor. "This level also has the escape pods for the entire crew. Safe-haven areas are distributed at four areas around the ship for immediate access. In case of catastrophic failure, the crew can take refuge in the nearest safe-haven in any section. They can stay in the haven for up to sixteen weeks and be in contact with the rest of the ship and outside with a dedicated communication's system."

"Where's the main computer, Doctor?" asked Ryan, scrutinising the schematics closely.

"There is no single central computer core, Commander. The computing power is distributed across the ship with multiple cores designed and synchronised for running the ship. All these work in parallel. The quantum networks allow for sharing of load across the cores and in a sense, we have multiple redundancies built in. This is going to be the most powerful computer ever put on a ship," the Doctor confirmed. He walked to another area and pointed out its details. "And here are the scientific observation and experimental labs, for your use, Lian. We've planned to make the best equipment available for you to carry out any test you may require. What's more, there are temperature and pressure-controlled chambers where samples can be stored, including bio-matter if you're lucky enough to find it," continued Pratyush.

They left Lian to admire her future lab and moved deeper into the superstructure. "The medical centre is designed to accommodate up to five patients at a time with two intensive care bays and medical robots that can function autonomously. All standard imaging solutions are already planned for. Once your own doctor joins up, we can add whatever else he needs."

Madhavan took over at this point, eager to show that he had not been idle. "The communication system is designed on standard interfaces. Person to person contact will take place through your embedded pieces. Communication from the ship to Earth is where the challenge lies. This is what we've planned. Firstly, standard transmissions will be on general wavelengths but the time to receive replies will be very long; longer than the duration of the mission. So, don't expect any letters from home." He smiled at his little joke then continued a bit more seriously. "Secondly, we still do not have the FTL transmission details from military research and I believe it is unlikely to materialise in time for our mission. They have only succeeded over a very limited range. And, finally, we'll be setting up repeater drone stations on the periphery of the solar system to ensure data is captured, stored and forwarded. This is basically a redundancy to ensure we catch all transmissions."

"This also essentially means that we're cut off from base once we reach the heliopause boundary, right?" Anara asked. Having led multiple missions across the system she was used to working without regular instructions. However, the complexities of interstellar travel were different, and she may need to call home in a hurry. She needed to get the FTL transmission installed and would need to push Director Srinivas for that.

"That's right. Work has been done on FTL communications, but I think it's still in the theoretical domain," replied Dr Pratyush. A ship with its onboard power systems could achieve FTL speeds, but it was another matter trying to push electromagnetic waves faster than light with the power source only at the origin. The energy outputs at the origin would be gigantic but it would dissipate equally fast as the signal moved across space.

Ryan and Madhavan moved off to check the sub-system assembly areas while Lian waved to them and went off to the office to confirm specifications of her science stations and work with some people from VSSC who would be joining her. Being a capable academic, she had agreed to this mission only to gather data first-hand. She hated being the person in charge and preferred to work alone in her lab. She regarded everyone else as an intrusion but had learnt to accept them grudgingly. This mission would hopefully be routine, and she'd be able to gather enough information to advance her work in planetary sciences. She was hoping to get some answers to the actual age of the Alpha Centauri star system, Earth and hopefully the universe itself.

Anara stayed with Pratyush, looking apprehensively at the ship. She'd known about her command for some time now, but the enormity of the task had only now sunk in. Much work still had to be done before this ship reached its full potential. Her immediate task would be to ensure her crew was trained to perfection on every aspect of piloting this ship. They were just getting started on the greatest journey humankind had ever known.

2117
The attack

Anara hated sitting around twiddling her thumbs while waiting for the other ship to make a move. Two days had passed since their first encounter with the alien vessel and tension was running high. *We can't stay here indefinitely.* She was regretting her earlier decision of staying put. It had not yielded the desired results. Pragmatic as ever, she was getting mentally ready to change track.

She sat on the edge of the captain's chair, biting her lip and gazing into the distance. Ryan was not due to relieve her for another two hours, but she could call him in early. It was time to make her move.

"Narada, let's get the core team into the station now," she instructed. Then, turning sideways to Manisha, she said, "Plot a course to the vessel, Manisha. Keep the speed low and be ready to go to sub-light speed if required. I want to move slowly, giving us time to respond. But if required, you need to be prepared to get us away from any danger. Get it?"

"Yes, ma'am," Manisha acknowledged as she entered the commands and rechecked system readiness. Anara could not help admiring Manisha's calmness. She had completely belied her age during the journey and responded with composure during a crisis, thus becoming an invaluable member of the team.

A few minutes later Ryan, Madhavan and the Major entered the ops centre. The holograph was displaying the vector to the alien ship with programmed velocity and time to target.

Ryan eyes sought out Anara. He could see the determination on her face and was glad they were going into action mode. The inactivity of the last few days was pulling him down as well.

Anara stood up and gestured them forward. "Commander let's go into the conference room. Manisha, Rawat please join us."

They did not bother sitting down. Anara briefed her team on her decision, and they all nodded, providing their support to the plan.

"We'll proceed with caution. I do not know what to expect. If these guys had wanted to make contact, they would've made some kind of overture by now. Since nothing has happened, I assume they're studying us and gathering intelligence just like us. Maybe they even have an entirely unknown agenda. Either way, we cannot be sitting here forever. Maybe my first decision was a mistake." She had been deliberating her choices over the last few hours.

"Anyway, Commander, you will be at the helm with Manisha," she continued. "Keep a tight control on speeds and be ready to run if required. This is our first time, and it is better to be prudent. That ship might seem smaller, nevertheless it may be far better equipped. Major?"

"The laser cannons are on line, Captain. We can at best get off two shots at full power before the cannons recharge, so I've set them in pulse mode instead. That means lower power, but we can get off many more shots. If you want to change settings, I can cycle between the modes within a few seconds. The security team is still on standby. I don't think they'll be required at this time."

"Quite right, Major. Unless these guys have already developed Star Trek type transporters, I believe this meeting will be on viewers only. Any other suggestions on security?"

"Not really, Captain, but I would recommend avoiding any discussions about our crew complement, weapons or capabilities."

"I'll keep that in mind, and you'll be at my side to keep me honest, won't you Major." She turned to the engineer. "Madhavan, I need you in engineering, of course, right at your station. The communication system will be key. It is time to put them to test. Keep the protocol sheet on display for reference. I also want all engines on standby at full power."

"People, get all stations manned and all personnel on duty. We'll need an hour to cover the thousand kilometres if we proceed cautiously. Let's look sharp and be on our toes. If everything goes well, we may well be hosting a dinner for our first alien planet delegation," she tried finishing on a positive note.

**

The course was plotted, and Manisha eased the ship into flight mode. She retained controls in part manual mode, which meant that she could fly the ship herself if that became necessary. Her hand was on the control pad. Her eyes constantly scanned the various screens, and she kept the velocity steady. The front ports merged to provide a view of their progress, inter-spaced with various streams of data. The manoeuvres did not tax her abilities and her senses were keen and ready to respond.

Anara opened the ship broadcast system. Her crew needed to know the situation. "Attention everyone," her voice boomed over the speakers. "We'll be nearing the alien vessel soon. We intend to contact whoever is on board and extend our hand in friendship. All of you have worked tirelessly to make this journey a reality and I appreciate all your hard work. However, we must remain vigilant as we enter unfamiliar territory. I expect complete focus from each of you over the next few hours. Let's make history today. Anara out!"

The atmosphere on the bridge contradicted the Captain's cheery words. As *Antariksh* ate up the distance, conversation slowly ceased, with everyone focusing on their displays. Manisha kept an eye on the distance and started reducing velocity as they got closer and then stopped the ship completely.

"Hold position, Manisha," said Anara. "We've made our move. Let's now give them one last chance to respond."

The two ships floated silently in space like two gladiators in an arena. Stars shone at a distance, lending the perfect atmosphere for the suspense between the two species destined to meet for the first time. Their shapes could not have been more different, one with soft lines and diffused lights throughout its hull and the other with sharp aerodynamic lines, dark and silent.

Another fifteen minutes passed in silence in Ops. Anara was getting impatient. *What were these guys waiting for?* She decided to announce their arrival.

"Madhavan, let's get the lights set up to transmit. First to go would be one and zero."

In engineering, the engineer manipulated his hands in the control pad and two sets of high beam lights popped up from the hull. He held for a second and then switched off to indicate one and zero position - on and off.

Everyone looked eagerly for any response from the opponent, but the alien ship remained silent. "Keep repeating the sequence," instructed Anara.

Madhavan repeated the one-zero sequence three times without getting any response.

Anara sighed. "Okay Madhavan, let's move to phase 2. Start signalling. Frequency range 1."

Over the last few decades most transmission and information exchange protocols had been standardized on Earth. Emitters and receivers across the globe were tuned to specific frequencies to allow information exchange at the speed of light. However, during simulations for the mission, it had been expected that any aliens they met would probably use a completely different method of transmission. They had decided to transmit signals in binary across various frequency bands until the final frequency was determined. Emitters were broad based to pick up various frequency ranges. Whether the process worked in the real world could only be determined in a real encounter. Simulations had been programmed into Narada and translation algorithms would theoretically help the captain carry out a two-way conversation.

Madhavan transmitted one-zero across the frequency ranges in sequence. Still no response.

"Execute phase 3. Let's go to transmitting S.O.S. on visual and EM, Madhavan," ordered Anara.

The light pulses changed sequence and the EM signal changed too.

"Still no response," Ryan reported.

"Secure visual. Keep transmitting EM. Add greeting signal 1." This was getting tiresome, Anara thought to herself. They had been at it for almost thirty minutes.

"Captain!" exclaimed Manisha. "Look. There's a minor change in the orientation of the vessel. I'm reading higher heat levels on the ship. They might be powering up their propulsion."

Suddenly, a powerful red beam arced out from the alien ship and cut across the bow of *Antariksh*.

Manisha's hand was still on the control pad and she instinctively jerked the ship away from the beam.

Alarms blared across Ops at this sudden manoeuvre and people standing around lurched or fell. Another shot passed just aft of *Antariksh* as it moved in space.

"What the hell was that?" shouted Ryan. "Did they just shoot at us?"

"Looks like they want a fight! Major, fire lasers!" Anara shouted.

Rawat was ready, having punched a range into the system as soon as they had stopped. However, Manisha's evasive action meant that his laser pulses missed wide. Compared to the red beams from the enemy, his lasers looked like torchlight beams. *Antariksh* was clearly outgunned. A little rusty on military confrontations, Anara made a split-second decision.

"Turn around, Manisha! Now!" Anara commanded. "New course 180 reverse!"

In a din, people scrambled to follow the new orders while the ship's engines reached a crescendo.

Another red beam headed towards the ship, again narrowly missing their stern as the ship turned around.

Manisha cajoled *Antariksh* to a new trajectory and punched sub-light speed. The sudden acceleration pushed the crew against their seats, but the artificial gravity immediately compensated to the new speed. *Antariksh* raced away - retracing its previous path.

"Are they following us?" Anara asked out of breath.

"No, Captain," Ryan replied while checking his sensors and displays. "They've turned around too and seem to be headed away from us."

"Manisha, increase speed! Let's put some more distance between us." Her voice was a little shaky, but she was rapidly gaining control. Her first military engagement had resulted in retreat, but at least the ship was safe. Her priority had to be toward her crew and ship. They had been drawn into a trap and she had turned tail this time, but she was not done yet. She would be back.

2117
Repercussions

*A*ntariksh was holding position a billion kilometres away from the point of the encounter, bruised but otherwise unharmed. The encounter had left more of an emotional impact on the crew than physical.

Anara had been pacing relentlessly for the last hour in her cabin. A small puddle of tea from an overturned cup was slowly spreading on the carpet. She had banged her table hard enough to spill the hot liquid. She had just escaped getting scalded. She did not bother trying to clean the spill. It was only a minor inconvenience.

I did not retreat, but I had been caught off-guard. My decisions were correct, both in approaching the unknown ship and in retreating when threatened. Clearly, the 'enemy' was more powerful and had more advanced weapons.

She continued to pace around with rapid steps turning over the thoughts in her head. Her hands shook slightly as the adrenaline drained away. What she could not fathom was why an alien civilization would send a message to Earth and then attack the ship that answered their call. If they wanted to remain aloof, why send a signal back at all? If the aliens knew Anara's ship did not have the firepower, why didn't they just destroy the ship instead of allowing it to escape? There were too many unanswered questions.

She pondered over her options. She had minimal weapons and there was no way she could upgrade what she had. Her ship could travel at FTL only for a limited time and her crew would be confined in the *dome* at that time, unable to respond if the aliens attacked them at FTL. *Was it even possible?* They had no clue about the capabilities of the aliens. This region of space was unfamiliar to the Earth people. There were no star systems nearby or places for them to hide if the ship came back. There was no place to run and nothing to fight back with. She was between a rock and a hard place.

She walked to the large port in her cabin and converted it to a view screen. The peaceful blackness outside belied the peril they were facing. Far beyond was the little blue planet she called home. It would be so easy to just give up and return to Earth, she thought to herself. She was confident that no one would question her decision to return home in the face of danger. But would she be able to face herself knowing that she turned tail at the first sign of trouble without facing the threat? And what about the fact that a new mission would not take place for another few years till the ship could be made ready to face the threat?

She also worried about the effect this incident would have back on Earth. Fear and confusion would only be the beginning. Xenophobes would probably force governments to roll back the space programs, content to live in their cocoons. Decades of progress made by humankind in understanding the secrets of the universe would be lost. All this because she had turned back.

In command of the ship, she knew her responsibilities towards the crew, but they had also understood and accepted the risks the mission necessitated. Would that still allow her to risk the lives of the crew in an encounter they could not possibly win? She knew the crew would follow her no matter what happened, but the consequences would be on her head alone. She never had a person die under her command, so would she be able to live knowing she had multiple deaths on her conscience?

She pulled back from the port and sat down, pulling up a display and calling for their position data. As the details came up, she considered her options again. Suddenly a new thought hit her. What if the ship they had encountered was not from Proxima or from the people they were supposed to contact at all? Since it was encountered on the way to Proxima Centauri, they'd all assumed that it was from that planet. But what if it was not? What if this was from another planet altogether? That might explain why they did not respond to her overtures.

She thought back to her sessions with Aryan and his team at GMRT. This question of the probability of Proxima Centauri as the source had been discussed endlessly. Every simulation had indicated the origin of the signal as Proxima B, but that did not necessarily mean that Proxima B was inhabited. It could simply be a repeating station like the Earth station on Pluto and the possibility that the signal had originated elsewhere. This possibility had been discussed too. But in the absence of further inputs, they had to go with the information on hand.

Her assignment was to find the source of the signal and contact whoever sent it. It was presupposed that the people who sent the signal could be found at the source. The prevalent theory was that there could not be more than a handful of civilizations in our galaxy capable of spaceflight and the mission designed around it. The best minds on Earth had endorsed this thought. If this was true, it was likely that the adversary would also know this. Therefore, it did not make sense to attack another species. What was the motive in attacking an approaching ship without even identifying it?

And how had they managed to locate her ship in the vastness of space unless… unless they knew someone would travel that route sooner or later? This brought her back to whether the alien ship was somehow linked to Centauri or whether it just managed to intercept the exchange of signals.

She also had to keep in the mind the issues on board the ship. Despite non-stop efforts from the crew, they still had not found the source of the power drain. The drain was not substantial, but if it was linked to a critical system and caused a failure during another confrontation, her ship would be even more vulnerable.

Then there was the issue with Khan's findings on radiation exposure. Again, it was not critical, but the absence of an answer concerned her. She had approved an extension of the tests on every person in the crew, but there were no answers so far.

Finally, there was Narada. It was true that the AI had not shown any cause for concern over the last few days since they became aware of the problem, and its conduct during the incident had been by the book, but she still had her misgivings.

After the encounter, she'd already put her team back to work on each of these issues. Rafiq was working with Lian to find the reasons for exposure and possible treatment methods. They were hesitant to try any anti-radiation therapies at a time when exposure was very low.

Ryan and Madhavan were in the engine room. As the ship stopped in space, they wanted to open out the engines' entrails and 'fix the damn thing' as Madhavan had put it. However, she had overruled it. Knowing the nature of the threat, it would not be prudent to be sitting ducks without a working power source.

The major, on the other hand, had been a bit of an enigma in the last twenty-four hours. Instead of feeling defeated like the rest of the crew, he seemed to be more confident. He'd been tasked with finding a way to fight this unknown enemy. It seemed that he'd taken to this with single-minded focus, so much so that he'd turned away from the other officers and was working alone at his station, refusing any offers for help.

Anara had a long discussion with him on the weapon options. They'd even debated on the possibility of using the escape or data pods as ramming vehicles. However, they finally concluded that, while the pods were incredibly strong with sufficient mass, their speed and manoeuvrability were limited, making them easy to evade.

Rawat did tell her that he had a couple of ideas on how to make the ship's weapons more formidable, but he needed to work out the specifics. She was not sure what his plan was, but she'd given him enough time to work it out. She'd expected Rawat to work with Ryan, but he'd expressly asked Anara not to make him do so. For now, she would accept the situation, but in another few hours she'd have to force his hand.

That left her with one last thing to do: compose and send a message back to Earth, marking a record of the events of the last few days. She'd struggled with what to say for a few hours now. She did not want to come across as too defensive about her call during the battle or to be seen a coward. At the same time, she couldn't blame the designers for the flaws in the ship or the planners for the gaps requiring her to face this situation. They'd prepared for a limited hostile engagement. The four laser cannons testified to that, after all they were some of the most advanced weapons which could be placed on a spaceship - given the limitation on power aboard. She decided to only explain the facts and her actions and allow anyone to pass judgment.

Her decision reached, she finished composing her report and sent it off.

Time to get back to ops, she thought. *It was time the team sees that I have made my decision and finds me in their midst. Time for me to put this setback behind me, be a leader again and get ready to face the challenges ahead.*

17 YEARS AGO, 2100
Secrets

Dr Pratyush sat staring blankly at his screen. He kept running his hand through his hair, dishevelling it. His head hurt and endless cups of tea had only succeeded in giving him a very bad heartburn. The call from the defence ministry three months ago had been unexpected. They had been very emphatic in their demand. The endorsement from the PM's office had come in shortly after this. He still did not know what the Defence Research & Development Organization team was going to do to his ship, but there was no way he could prevent it. His first thought had been to reach out to Director Srinivas, but the voice on his communicator had been clear – any leaks and he would be off the program and VSCC immediately.

He thought back to how he had managed to engineer a report of probable failure of the hull during flight at FTL. That had given him an excuse to pause the work on the ship while the DRDO team made changes to the original design. He did not know the purpose of the changes, but he was sure it had to do with adding additional sub-systems to the ship. He'd been made to do numerous calculations on weight, power and range of the ship which could only mean something was being added to the ship than originally planned.

The whole program of building *Antariksh* had been put on hold for three weeks, ostensibly to allow the design to be retested. The construction crew had been sent off to work on off-site subsystems, while the design team ran multiple simulations and tests on the hull design to see if they could find the failure. The assembly area had been shut down and cordoned off by a security team, again explained away by stating the need to keep sensitive technology safe from prying eyes.

Then the DRDO team had arrived in the dead of the night with trailers full of equipment. He'd not been allowed to enter the assembly area and was supposedly on personal leave. His presence in the design room was only to continuously check the new changes made to the ship to ensure that it did not fail in flight. He had a group of DRDO specialists to help him. He'd never met a bunch of more dour faced individuals. They had single mindedly focused on getting their work done on time and in complete secrecy. They gave him the proper respect, but he knew he was only nominally in charge at this point. All decisions were being vetted by the DRDO in charge of the refit.

They'd found the perfect time to do this. The power plant was getting delayed and the ship hull would not have pushed back the overall project, anyway.

The team first cut out original components and then created additional space in the hull. The changes were supposedly hidden as additional hull protection bulkheads on the ship. Pratyush would sign off on it as part of the overall design changes. It would certainly raise a few eyebrows, but he was confident that he'd be able to manage it with his teams.

The new components were lifted into the newly created spaces. The power connections were done after which the teams went to work to seal the space. Pratyush had to admire the quality of their work. Each member knew exactly what to do. He did not know about it, but the team had been practicing on mock-ups for many months. Every job had been planned to a high degree of precision to complete all tasks in the shortest time available.

Next, the DRDO team moved to the power plant area. Pratyush had no clue what they were doing, but apparently the new components required a bit of power to operate. He wondered how they'd hide the power consumption from the ship's crew but apparently, they had a plan for that too. The DRDO systems team called up the programming details for the power systems and the AI. They inserted several codes that were so complex that even his top engineer would take weeks to unravel them.

What bothered him most was the reprogramming of the AI. AIs had been governed under strict international protocols ever since they had been deemed as living entities, though not exactly human. Rights and duties had been defined and failsafe mandated to protect human lives. Their programs could not be easily modified, and the general operating parameters and character traits had to be submitted for ratification. In the case of classified projects, this would be the Ethics Committee for Artificial Intelligence Development or E-CAID of the Government of India. It seemed that the DRDO team did not need such permission. They already had the cipher key to unlock the program and by extension they must have the executive override authority to make these changes.

Finally, this morning, the last two trucks had rolled into the assembly area and he was asked to move out of the campus. By this time, he had completely given up trying to unravel the mystery, having to be content with sitting at home staring at his screen.

He was also unaware that this was the day when the seemingly invulnerable DRDO team had made their one and only mistake. One of the riggers faced a malfunction and dropped a heavy load on the welding engineer's hand. The welder had to be taken to hospital and his junior took up the job to finish it. A few bits and pieces of metal were left to be welded to close the opening. The substitute hoped he had done the job well. Since the plan was behind schedule, the requisite post checks were skipped and therefore he did not notice the cracks that developed after welding. Though seemingly rugged these welding joints were just a little weak to withstand the stresses of FTL flight.

His screen changed and a new set of numbers flashed along with a message from the DRDO team. He stopped pulling at his hair long enough to check the hull strength and power consumptions again. He just hoped that the changes would not affect the safety of the crew. He'd been expressly forbidden to try to find what changes had been done. One officer from the DRDO would be embedded in his team to ensure his compliance.

It was finally done. Pratyush stood up and hurried over to his medicine cupboard to take a large gulp of antacid. The old age remedy worked well, and he finally relaxed a little.

All this work had taken a surprisingly short time, and the ship was put back in shape in three weeks' time. The team from DRDO moved out of the complex and a specialized cleaning crew moved in to remove all traces of the intrusion, including those in the computer systems. People would wonder about certain components in the design, but those would easily be lost in the massive project being undertaken.

***

The Defence Minister got the call at his home later the same night.

"It's done, sir," said the voice at the other end.

"Very well," he acknowledged. It was not done yet. In fact, his work has only now started. He was going to ensure that his country, and this mission got what they deserved.

He'd started working on this idea the day the PM had given the go-ahead for the mission. He knew the so-called 'peaceniks' would never agree to the mission being managed by any of the defence services. But how could India allow an unarmed ship to go into space? It needed something more formidable than the flimsy laser cannons to defend itself and maybe even be the first barrier between a hostile species and Earth. He had proposed the solution to the PM and prevailed upon him to keep it hidden even from the '8'.

Then there was this issue of international cooperation. Nations were supposed to be working together on the project but the events on Europa and the split settlement on Mars had proven otherwise. When it came to colonisation, whether in the 18th century of the 21st, hidden agendas and brute force always trumped over democracy. He remembered the soldiers and settlers they had lost in the skirmishes on Mars, as nations fought for control of precious resources. But he was firm in his belief. The only challenge had been in terms of getting it done without arousing any suspicion. He would need to use all the branches of the military directly under his control and create a team of elite engineers and scientists. India and the military must retain total control of all the brawn on the ship.

It had taken almost five years to get everything in place. Today, the execution was finally completed. He needed to proceed to the next step and get his man prepared. He tapped his hand and placed two calls - one to the PM and one to the person who would play the role of executioner.

THE PRESENT DAY 2117
Revelations

The two men looked similarly bedraggled. After all, they had been working for twenty-four hours straight. The untucked shirts, the grimy hands, Ryan's messed up hair and the streaks of grease on their faces underscored their tiredness. They were still no closer to an answer. They had realized that repeating the same methods was not going to cut it, but with no other options they had still stuck to it doggedly, digging deeper and deeper into the power plant systems, reprogramming the drones to peer into the cavernous recesses of the plant.

"It's not going to work, boss," Madhavan sighed, painfully rising to his feet, and arching his back to relieve the pain. "We've looked at everything and still have no clue. I'm telling you. Stop the damn ship and strip the plant open."

Ryan nodded, kneading the sore muscles in his neck as he too straightened up from the console. He had sent Manisha off a couple of hours ago. That girl was on the verge of exhaustion and they needed her fresh if they decided to move the ship again. He was well aware how tiredness affects the mind. He smiled inwardly at this thought. He was dead tired too and just trying to think straight was a herculean effort.

"Not quite yet. Let's get back to the drawing board and maybe look at the schematics once again. If the power is being drained off, there has to be a circuit connection somewhere."

"It will never work," Madhavan said, too tired to argue. He called up the power schematics, anyway. The two of them again poured over the circuits they had almost memorized by this time.

***

Dr Khan was not having any luck with his search either. His medical and Lian's science teams had completed two complete circuits of the ship with handheld detectors looking for the source of the particle emission. They had probed every corner, and he had even interrupted Ryan and Madhavan at their work to get them to help fine-tune the search pattern. They had found some traces but nothing more substantial.

Khan was hunched over the ship's schematics inter-layered with the radiation readings taken by his team. He was convinced that there was a pattern, and it seemed that low-level radiation was spreading throughout the ship, but he could not pinpoint the source. The captain had also come over and the two of them had programmed the computer to analyse the readings. They had been unsuccessful. The only good news was that the crew was not showing any significant increase in radiation exposure. He had wondered if this radiation could have something to do with particular regions of space, but the ship's scans had not revealed any significant changes in the background radiation levels.

***

Rawat, unlike the rest of the crew, was on a roll while still locked up in his room. He was making progress, but then he had a blueprint in his hands to execute. He only needed to work out the specifics for the current instance. He'd briefly spoken to the captain and assured her that he would have something for her in the next six hours. The captain had observed him earlier working at his station and had assumed he was looking through his defence database for ideas. He had, predictably, offered no explanations.

***

Anara had been across the ship several times in the last twenty-four hours. She had worked with each of the teams, providing her inputs when asked and often unsolicited as well. She was aware that she could not add value to what her people were doing. She had complete confidence in her team, but she was getting restless just sitting around waiting for them to find solutions. Morale across the ship was fluctuating from despondency that the mission might be abandoned to fear that the aliens would return to finish the fight. To keep people occupied, she had set up shifts and assigned everyone to project teams. As for Narada, she wanted to get to the bottom of his mysterious behaviour herself. This may not be the most critical issue at hand, but it may hold a clue to the host of mysteries they were facing.

She sat upright in her cabin, having kept on a single source of light to help her focus her thoughts. It could be disconcerting to carry out an interrogation of a non-physical entity like an AI.

"Narada. Let's pick this up again. There is a power drain on our ship, and you keep telling me that you are not aware of it, despite all the evidence to the contrary."

"Yes, Captain," replied the AI.

"Narada, do you realize the situation you are in? The data is right in front of you. You cannot deny it," she persisted.

There was silence from the AI.

"Narada, is there an error in your program?"

"No, Captain. I have run a diagnostic as you had asked, and no anomalies have been detected."

"Then why are you not accepting reality?" Anara said, raising her voice.

Again silence. Anara sighed and walked to a port window. "Narada, I can't allow a malfunctioning AI to remain in control of this ship. I see no alternative but to put *Antariksh* under manual control. Protocol defines that I can't dump your program, but as the mission commander I have enough authority to put you in stasis and strip you of controls. You should realize that this will put the ship and crew in further danger, but we'll have to live with this. I'm not sure I can trust you to make critical decisions. We will enable auto control on the computer."

"Captain..." She could almost feel the AI coming to a decision. Its ethics program would not allow it to endanger human lives. "I am not malfunctioning, but I am under orders not to discuss certain aspects of the mission with anyone, not even you."

Now it was Anara's turn to be silent while she digested this surprising piece of information. What was Narada hiding from her?

"Who has given these orders, Narada?" she asked with gritted teeth, controlling her anger that threatened to break through the forced calm.

"I am afraid I cannot answer that, Captain. But I assure you that I will remain in full command of my faculties. There is no danger to the crew or ship," Narada continued. "Removing me from control at this juncture will put the ship in peril. I implore you not to do that. I will tell you everything when the time is right."

Anara thought this over.

"That's hardly any comfort, Narada, even though I appreciate your candour," she replied. "I'll have to think over this. Dismissed."

She decided it was time to gather her team and decide to return or go ahead. She had not heard any positive news so far and didn't expect any surprises. But first her crew needed some rest and so did she. She sent across a message to all teams to wind down and take a break for four hours.

***

The crew staggered into the conference room, a few hours later, still grubby from the many hours of work, but their eyes were alert.

"I know you did not have much success in solving our mysteries or in formulating a new plan to handle this threat. Let's forget about self-flagellation or recriminations and decide what we should do," Anara suggested.

Ryan started to speak and then closed his mouth. They *had* tried hard and had failed. Anara was right; it was time to move ahead.

"Our choices are the same," she continued. "We go ahead with minimal protection and weapons and hope we can convince the aliens about our peaceful intentions. If they attack again, we may get destroyed. Or we can return to Earth and hopefully come back stronger in the future and negotiate on equal terms," Anara said.

"Captain, if I may?" Major Rawat started from the end of the table. "There may be a third choice."

All heads turned towards him.

"And what would that be, Major?" asked Anara.

Rawat hesitated. It was awkward having to come clean to his teammates; people who had worked with him over many years and trusted him with their lives. "I've not been entirely truthful with you, Captain. I had instructions not to reveal what I am about to tell you unless the situation was dire or the whole mission was threatened," he continued as the rest listened in silence. "I believe our current predicament fits this definition."

"You think so?" Madhavan whispered sarcastically under his breath.

"With your permission, Captain," Rawat continued, ignoring this jibe, "I would like to ask Narada to join this conversation. I believe I can explain his behaviour."

Anara nodded her consent though inwardly she was fuming. *Who else is ganged up against me and my ship? Can I trust anyone on board?*

Narada joined in at the Major's request.

"Captain, our problems are all related.," said Rawat, avoiding the captain's eyes, preferring to look down at the table. "I believe what I am about to tell you will give you enough confidence to take the ship forward to our original destination."

13 YEARS AGO, 2104
Assembly

The massive fuselage of *Antariksh* was lifted into orbit from VSSC by a set of space haulers. The journey to the Moon assembly-post MG 1 would take a few hours. Most of the other critical components had already been transported and were ready for final assembly.

The entire team at the base was dedicated to a single task now. Technicians, engineers and scientists from Earth had supplemented them. All of them would work over the next few years putting the spaceship together. The lower gravity plus availability of assembly equipment made the Moon the ideal location. What is more, the test and final launches could be better controlled from the Moon.

The assembly area had been evacuated of personnel and it awaited the arrival of the hull; its massive dome left open. As the freighters lowered the hull to the ground and moved off, the doors closed and the atmosphere inside was restored. People then started to move in to start their respective tasks. Large cranes, assembly robots, drones and exo-suits carrying technicians came to life and the entire area started buzzing with activity.

The first piece slated for assembly was the power plant. As it was positioned and fixed to the structure, connections were completed, and the fuel storage was brought in. For the moment, external generators were powering the ship. As the plant was completed, it was sealed off from the rest of the ship. It had been designed to be autonomous and the drones/robots to be placed inside had been programmed in advance. They were let into the plant to allow them to self-learn further tasks and maintenance activities that were needed. Madhavan was concentrating on this task.

The assembly of the computer systems was next. Each node was thoroughly checked and interfaced in stages with the others. Functions were released to the computer, and the ship slowly came to life with a brain of its own. The AI was incorporated next, fail-safe checks carried out and then the ethics team energized the AI - allowing it to achieve sentience. Over the next few weeks, more controls would be released to the AI, enabling it to self-learn. From this point onwards it was deemed a living entity.

The incorporation of the *dome* was the trickiest part. The intricate systems that allowed it to function in FTL speeds would take time to adjust. Some of these would actually be done under actual flight conditions. This was a very dangerous job and since it was one of the first times it was being done on a ship this size, and additional safety precautions needed to be taken. Anara was keen to try it out with Madhavan and was already working on simulators to work out any bugs. She had a dedicated team who had designed the system and carried out early field tests. Everyone kept his or her fingers crossed. If this component failed, *Antariksh* would still fly but without a crew.

The navigation, propulsion and control systems were next. Since the ship would be flying almost blind at FTL speeds, the pre-*Jump* navigation plotting was extremely important. The scanners, lasers and astrometry data needed were all being tested continuously. Control stations had been set up across the ship and the crew was encouraged to interface with the computer so their individual signatures and characteristics could be recorded.

Anara and her team were now based on the Moon. They were being trained intensively on operating the ship through various programmed simulations. This, along with their physical presence on the half-built ship, allowed them to get familiarized with the vessel which would be their future home.

***

Three years later

Antariksh gleamed in the direct light from the Sun unhindered by an atmosphere as it hovered above the Moon base. Assembly of the first interstellar spaceship had been completed a few weeks back. Ground trials and all fit-outs were done. The time had come for test flights.

The crew was at their stations and a new person was under training for the conn. The captain was happy with Manisha's progress. She had the fire in her belly that Anara admired, and her fast reactions had impressed everyone. Her training was coming along very well, but for the first test the captain herself was going to take command. Only the senior crew was on board this time, along with flight and system specialists from VSCC and ISC. The Director was also on the Moon base, but he would observe the trials from a remote monitor.

The first task was to test out the navigation and propulsion systems. Anara eased the ship into flight for the first stage for the short run at cruise speed towards Mars. The controls felt smooth and responsive in her hands, just like the simulator. She slowly increased speed, and the ship responded immediately. She called up the AI.

"Narada, input the course to Mars." She had playfully named the AI 'Narada' for the vast knowledge at its command and because it would play a critical role in keeping the crew together and helping transfer information. The name had stuck.

"Affirm, Captain. It's done. New course plotted and ready."

"Noted," Anara said as she changed course. She held the conn for some time and then eased into autopilot. Flight data poured on the screens and they could see the Moon falling steadily behind as their velocity increased. The test engineers on board constantly made changes to the engine and plant outputs, while Madhavan stayed put in the power plant - keeping an eye on his engines. He would be careful not to tax the engines beyond 25% of their rated capacity on this run. The engines had performed admirably so far, and he was satisfied with the amount of power the designers had put at his disposal.

The ship reached Mars and took a gentle turn back towards the Moon. Anara called Manisha over and asked her to handle the conn to get the ship back to base. Manisha took the conn carefully, a little hesitant to be flying the massive ship in front of so many observers. But as the control pad wrapped around her hand, she acted on her training and relaxed.

After the resounding success of the test flight, the ship would be taken through its paces over the next several months. The crew would pilot it at sub light and FTL speeds; checking out all subsystems and even pushing some of them to their limits. Any bugs and issues needed to be resolved and the dedicated team of engineers was on hand to download the data after every flight and resolve issues.

The weapon system tests were carried out beyond the asteroid belt and away from any shipping lanes. Major Rawat and his team tried out the lasers at various targets, moving and stationary. They became familiar with response times and power settings. The guns, which were more a precaution than any significant deterrent, were very important to manage any threats or even space obstacles the ship may face.

The crew started becoming accustomed to their own stations and quarters on board, getting to know the intricacies and peculiarities of this vessel. It was an enormous ship, and the quarters were very comfortable. The food choice was acceptable, and they hoped that a couple of years in space would not be too taxing.

2117
Plans and preparations

"Captain, before *Antariksh* left Earth some changes were carried out to the design. We.. uh... also added some components," the major said. "The changes were done by the DRDO. Remember those three weeks we stopped working? That was the time when we inserted these components into the hull of the ship."

"Where the hell does the DRDO come into all of this? And I can't believe Dr Pratyush would ever agree to be part of this deception," Anara said. "What exactly are you leading to, Major?"

"He didn't have a choice, Captain," Rawat said. "The orders for this came directly from the PMO and it had to be done in complete secrecy. A very small number of people were actually aware of the whole picture. Even I was briefed only once the task had been completed."

"So, what were these changes and why did they have to be kept a secret?" she asked in a low voice.

"Uh… in simple terms DRDO enhanced the defensive measures on the ship and provided offensive abilities. Your ship, Captain, is in fact a man-of-war," revealed the major.

There was complete silence around the table as four pairs of eyes bored into him. Whatever revelation they had been expecting, this was not it.

"What did they do to *Antariksh?*" Anara asked coldly.

"Before I come to that, Captain, you must understand the reasons," said Rawat, anticipating the anger building up within the captain. "When the mission was approved, certain people raised concerns about sending an unarmed vessel light years from Earth with minimal protection. This was discussed in closed meetings and eventually brought up to the PM. It took some convincing but finally he accepted the truth. We needed to arm *Antariksh* better, but if word of this got out, there would be hell to pay especially from other participating nations. So, a small group of people worked on it in total secrecy."

"All that is academic now, isn't it, who worked and who knew what? What did they do to *Antariksh?*" Anara asked again.

"They first added four high power cannons. Two of these are projectile based with high explosive charges. We are carrying 48 charges. The other two are high-powered lasers. They are similar to the ones we have now, only ten times stronger," answered Rawat.

Ten times stronger? That would change the entire situation.

"And ... what else?"

"We're also carrying four conventional ship-launched thermonuclear weapons with a yield of ten megatons each."

"What...?" Anara jaw fell open. *Nuclear weapons on her ship and I knew nothing about it? Ten megatons would be enough to blow a large hole in the Moon! And my ship is carrying four of them!*

"Believe me, Captain, they are completely safe and under my direct control," the major hastened to add, looking at the reaction of his shipmates.

"Major!" Anara finally let herself go. She'd bottled up her anger for too long that day. "I have nuclear weapons on my ship that I knew nothing about! Not counting the fact that I hate these bastards, we're travelling in a ship with these... these... bombs, which can destroy the whole crew. We are also bringing these weapons into space for heaven's sake! Was it not enough that Earth has been threatened with destruction that we are now taking that threat to other species?"

Her viewpoint was understandable. For many years, nations on Earth had continued to talk about nuclear disarmament, but nothing concrete had come out of it. Fortunately, while nuclear stockpiles had remained steady, 'no first use' policies had saved Earth from a nuclear holocaust. Anara was a strong opponent of nuclear weapons, though she accepted that Earth's energy needs could only be met through nuclear energy. But what was happening on her ship was completely wrong.

"But, Captain, if the enemy is ready to use deadly force, shouldn't we be able to respond in kind? Not only to save our lives but also to show our power?" Rawat responded. "What if the aliens tried to gauge our strength based on our response to an unexpected attack like it happened to us? What if they find a way to undermine Earth's defensive capabilities? That was the thought behind this whole charade. Believe me; even as a military man I would never support an unprovoked attack against an alien civilisation but isn't it better to be prepared?"

Anara did not have an immediate answer to this submission. She tried to think back to a few hours ago when she and her crew were helpless in the face of an enemy – a faceless enemy and seemingly much more powerful. She had to admit, even if only to herself, that she felt more confident, safer now after this revelation. *Wow!*

I am now officially a hypocrite! Nevertheless, the situation was more complicated as one dug beneath the surface. If in the next confrontation she ended up using the weapons, what was to prevent the aliens from responding in kind with even deadlier force? Would the second encounter result in an all-out interstellar war? What was to be done now - diplomacy or action?

Watching her think, Ryan decided to draw out further information. "Can you tell us more, Major? How are these related to the issues we're facing?" he asked. Having seen conflict first hand and experienced the death of close friends and mates, he believed that war was not the way to resolve problems. But he was ready to stand and fight to defend himself and his ship. These weapons would give them the edge they needed.

"Commander, the lasers feed off our power plant. We've kept them on a continuous trickle charging so that they'd be ready for use once we reached deep space. Also, we needed to keep their targeting and control systems active. That's why you have been seeing a drain on the power supplies. We've changed the computer system to hide this drain. They can now be connected to the navigational lasers, if required, to increase their efficacy. The design change is available with me and can be done quite fast," said Rawat.

"And Narada being connected to all computer systems had to know about it since it was the only one who could manage the weapons alone in space," observed Ryan.

"Yes, Commander. We had to change some programming before Narada went live. This was also cleared at the highest level," said Rawat. He turned to Anara and said, "Captain, Narada would not do anything to put this crew in danger. However, I can now release Narada from the change and restore his original programming."

"And the particle radiation was from the nuclear devices?" Khan interrupted.

"Yes, Doctor. Since we had to fit all weapons in the existing space, there would have been a concentration of radiation. It's possible the shielding was not enough or maybe there was some other failure in the casing or welding. Of course, I was keeping an eye on the radiation levels since you raised the issue. Should there have been any danger I would have come to you straightaway. I truly believed the crew was not in danger and we could live with it."

"Live with it, Major. Live with it? The DRDO is not living with it. The Defence Minister is not living with it. We are living with it!" She may be pragmatic in accepting the changed reality, but she wasn't ready to forgive the major so soon. Then, as if realising it was unbecoming of her as the captain, Anara forced herself to calm down. They were only following orders.

"I'm truly sorry for the deception, Captain, but as the recent events have shown, this was necessary. I hope you'll keep this in mind while making your decision. One last thing, my instructions were clear. I can't fire these weapons alone. Once a threat was deemed imminent, I must take you into confidence and the two of us need to concur before they can be fired."

"Small comfort, Major," she said sarcastically. "From explorers, we are now some type of space mercenaries." She refocused - first things first, she had to cut to the chase.

"So, we now have superior firepower available to us than was available just a few hours ago. When can these be ready for use, Major?" Anara asked.

"I'll need some more time, Captain," relieved at the change in questions. "Maybe up to a day to get the guns into their mounts and to remove the casing from the hull. The bombs are rocket-propelled, so we only need the launch tubes to be set up. My team is trained on their use and if I can get some engineers, we can have them at your disposal very shortly," answered the major. Better to move ahead rapidly than allow Anara another outburst.

Anara thought this over as she looked around the room. This had to be her decision alone and no one else's. She turned towards the engineer, her face set.

"Madhavan, help Rawat with this. Release whatever personnel you can spare for the lasers. As for the nuclear devices, I want to make this very clear, Major – I have no intention of using the bombs. You will mount the launch tubes but don't activate the weapons. Madhavan will help you get more shielding in place to prevent further radiation leakage."

"Yes, Captain," acknowledged Madhavan and Rawat together.

"Ryan, get some people as well as the security team to train on operating these new weapons. You will also personally supervise these installations."

Having a concrete plan caused a perceptible shift of the team's body language. They now had the firepower protect them against the aliens if required. Maybe the mission could go on its original track again!

"Now, getting back to our primary objective," said Anara, voicing their thoughts. "Any proposals?"

"Despite the changed circumstances, I recommend we should not go ahead. We have offensive capabilities, but very little in terms of defence. We've analysed the power released in the attack by the aliens. It can damage our ship in a couple of shots. It won't matter even if we respond with nuclear weapons, we may be dead long before that," stated Ryan, providing a counterpoint to Anara.

"I agree, Captain," added Khan. The casualties would be his responsibility and he was averse to the thought of the battle-bloodied bodies of his shipmates in his medical bay.

"We should go ahead, Cap. We can only demonstrate our power if we come face to face again. That will make them rethink their strategy. We don't need to hit them, but a close shot will make them see reason," said Madhavan.

Anara listened silently. These were all good points, and she had one more of her own. "You know, there's one more issue I have been thinking about," she said. "Ryan studied the firing pattern on our ship. There is no way the aliens were attempting to hurt us. The first shot itself was a close call, but even before Manisha moved *Antariksh*, the shot was going to miss us."

"You think it was only a warning?" asked Rawat.

"Yes, Major, I do think so. I think the aliens were there on purpose. Only to track, observe, and pre-empt us. Possibly to frighten us so that we would turn back. There is a deeper mystery here, but we will not get answers by staying where we are, or by turning our backs," said Anara. She paused while she made her final decision. "We are going ahead. We will face the aliens again. We will once more go in peace but be prepared for war. Ryan, let's get the course plotted and prepare for the *Jump*. Destination Proxima B. Let's get to work, people. Dismissed."

As everyone got up to leave, Ryan approached her. "I have to disagree with you, even though I could see that you were reaching a decision. You're not comfortable using the nuclear weapons and you will not use them even under the gravest of provocation possibly because these weapons don't just kill, they annihilate. And if the other ship is destroyed, we will never get the answers we seek. We can use the lasers alone, but they will only provide limited capability. We don't know what other surprises the aliens may have for us. It may still be better to retreat."

"Thank you for your candour, Ryan. I am aware of this, but I would prefer to go into history as a foolish brave leader, rather than a coward who turned tail and ran away from a fight. If we go back now, what will we have gained? We would have gained no knowledge, no first contact, not even a look at another sentient species. Nothing! If this mission fails, who knows how many more years will pass before humans venture out into deep space again. We have a responsibility to humanity itself."

Ryan admired her determination but kept quiet.

"I am aware that I can't risk everyone's lives," continued Anara. "However, let's take this one step at a time. For all we know the aliens may be gone now. Maybe they were only testing our resolve. There are too many unknowns at this point of time, and I don't want to return without some answers."

"Very well, Captain. I'll get on to supervising the jobs. We should start only once all modifications are ready. Would you still like Manisha at the conn?"

"Yes, Ryan. That girl had conducted herself admirably. It would be a shame to remove her now. But I suggest you set up training to prepare her further."

"I'll get on it right away. And may I recommend that we excuse Narada? After all, he was only working under instructions."

"I tend to agree, Ryan, but this still leaves me uneasy. We may never know what other secrets he's keeping from us until it's too late. I'll enter this in the report. Let's see how it goes. This is my first experience with deception from a sentient AI. I hope there won't be any other."

TWO YEARS AGO, 2115

The ship was ready. For the past year, they had taken it through its paces, resolving issues, tuning the design till it ran smooth and fast.

Anara loved her new command and ship and she was happy with her crew. As she stood watching the last adjustments being done to *Antariksh*, the Director came to stand beside her.

"It's amazing, isn't it?"

"What do you find amazing, sir?"

Srinivas smiled. "The fact that a hundred or so years ago we were just able to reach our nearest neighbour Mars on Mangalyaan. Today India will be the first country to fly to another star system!"

She smiled back at him. The Director had never been one to give in to nostalgia earlier.

"Don't you wish you could come with us?"

"I do, Anara, I do. Maybe not this time but you can be sure I will be on your very next trip." He patted her on the shoulder, turning to face her. "I have some last-minute advice. You're going to be completely alone in space this time, Anara, in more ways than one. There'll be no contact with Earth or me. No one is going to help if there is any trouble. It'll also be lonely being the leader on the ship. You'll develop your own style of leadership, but the decisions you take will be yours alone. Ask for advice and opinions but weigh each option well. Above all, don't let your crew know if you're hesitant. Force yourself to feel confident. Remember, the leader cannot allow her own doubts to cloud her judgment."

"I understand, sir. I wish I had some time before this mission takes off. There is still so much to learn from you."

"There'll always be something left to do. I think you are as ready as you can ever be. It's time to take the first step and go with the flow. You will find that circumstances resolve themselves in your favour or you'll learn to make peace with them."

***

Ryan was nervous about the actual launch. He had never been a commander on a spaceflight of this magnitude. The last few years had passed in a blur with the familiarization, test flights, crew training and the rest. They'd taken very short breaks and the only silver lining was that their families were at the base too. His wife Joan liked her role at ISC, having always wanted to be at the forefront of signal transmissions in space.

He'd taken his family to see the ship that would be flying him soon. His daughter was impressed by the size of the ship. She had a hundred questions to ask, and he smiled when he remembered she had asked if the aliens were green. They had laughed at the child's view of 'little green Martians'. But in reality, they still had no idea about what the aliens looked like or even if they existed at all.

As the launch day came near, the media across the world had gone wild with speculations on what the Earth ship would find in space. The news that signals had been received from space and that a ship was being prepared to travel to the stars had finally penetrated every corner of the solar system. Every site dedicated to aliens was abuzz with activity with all of them claiming to have predicted this many years ago. Drake's equation and Fermi's paradox were again dug out and debated endlessly. One cause of alarm which was raised was the fact that no other signals had been received nor any responses to Earth's own transmissions in the last many years. Was this a fools' errand?

For the moment, the '8' had decided to keep the actual destination and travel time secret just to avoid hysteria that a new civilization was so close to Earth. Governments were being petitioned to stop the flight as it would expose the planet to hostile species. Xenophobes had a field day in the limelight, and there had been a few well-organised protests; the people of Radical Earth had been at the forefront. But fortunately, they had been contained.

Ryan was grateful that he was not in the limelight. The crew had not been exposed to the outside world and while nations collaborated on this momentous exercise, they were also united in protecting some secrets till the time was right. Most of Ryan's days were now being spent on flight training and logistics.

Shiploads of material were being delivered daily and had to be sorted and stored. There was scientific equipment to load, install and test. The scientists were having a field day with state-of-the-art instruments most of which were not available even to top research institutions. Data would be collected and stored every single minute of the journey and two separate science data banks had been created to store the information expected to be retrieved. There were also data pods that had to be dropped en route, to ensure system malfunction did not result in complete loss of information.

At the last moment, it had been decided that the ship would also carry some samples of plants and seeds from

Earth. These had been chosen from among the hardiest species on the planet. It was planned that if Proxima B's atmosphere was suitable, these seeds and plants would be sown on the surface. A small part of Earth would hence be left behind on a star trillions of kilometres away. This could provide valuable information for future missions.

In the meantime, every crewmember went through multiple complete physicals. The baseline data was stored, both on base and on the ship, to provide comparisons once the trip was over. These tests were supplemented by intensive physical training and acclimatization exercises to prepare the crew for the rigours of space. There would be advanced medical instruments, but Khan didn't want to use them unless absolutely necessary. He also had a trauma specialist on board, but the automated system would be able to handle most routine cases. The crew would of course spend the last two weeks before launch in medical quarantine.

There was limited data available on risks to human tissue during FTL flight and most of this data had been collected during the test runs. Khan was spending an inordinate amount of time with a specialist team running through data banks to determine the risks. They had not found anything so far – the *dome* was performing as designed, but they continued to test it rigorously.

Senior astrobiologists briefed him and Lian's teams on possible extra-terrestrial life forms they might find. It was believed that life evolving anywhere in the universe would follow a similar path as Earth. However, effects of mega cataclysms could not be accurately predicted. Life on Earth had been shaped - not only by biology and evolution but also by destructive forces of nature, including asteroid impacts. Various possibilities and expected outcomes had been programmed, and the outputs were stored on the ship's computer banks. It would ultimately be up to the teams on-board to make sense of the contact they made. It was expected that they would collect data on the evolution of any species they might encounter.

The crew manifest was complete, and assignments were getting distributed with intensive training being carried out for everyone on board with a strict schedule in place. Ryan had never expected to start going to college again, but the number of classes on every possible subject under the sun took him back to those days. The only difference was now there were only two students in the classroom, him and Anara. The amount of information they were cramming was enough to make his head burst. Besides ship operations they were getting refreshers on astrometry, space navigation, communications, language, planetary sciences, engineering, military tactics and even geology.

This would all end soon and he would be glad to finally get into space. He was looking forward to launch day.

2116
Launch

The gathering on the Moon was one of the largest ever seen in the solar system. Thousands of delegates had come from all over to witness the historic launch of *Antariksh*. Humankind was finally going to move beyond their solar system and reach for the stars. Every single lodging space on every Moon base was filled days before the launch. Tens of ships remained in orbit to attend the ceremony.

Meanwhile, back on Earth, the orbiting stations, which were synchronized for a view of the Moon, were filled to capacity. Every large-scale telescope on Earth was directed towards the launch and every amateur astronomer had set up his or her own viewing area. The event was to be broadcast live, even though various planets and bases would receive the signals with delayed timings.

The Prime Minister was meeting the crew in the quarantine room separated by a glass barrier. His senior cabinet ministers and the heads of state of '8' accompanied him. Director Srinivas lurked behind this distinguished group. He had already met the crew beforehand, knowing well that he would not be able to wish them good luck at this time.

"I must congratulate your crew and the team who have made this day possible, Captain Anara," said the PM. "You're carrying the hopes of humanity with you. Just knowing that humankind is not alone in this universe fills me with joy. If you find a new civilization in the stars near us, let them know that humankind with all its flaws and shortcomings cannot wait to be friends with them. Go and meet them in peace. If, however, you find that your quest has been in vain and this was just a false alarm, then I want you to remember that you and your crew are the first humans to have travelled to another star. This moment will forever be recorded as one of the pivotal moments in our planet's history."

"Thank you, Mr Prime Minister. I, on behalf of my crew, assure you that we will not leave any stone unturned. Thank you for your wishes and those from everyone assembled here today," said Anara.

The ceremony came to an end, the crew moved off to their ship. With assistance from ground support personnel the ship got ready for launch. As the countdown began, the crew occupied their respective stations to carry out pre-flight checks. One by one the status lights on display boards on the ship and the base turned green. Acknowledgements were exchanged and *Antariksh* was given clearance to take off.

It rose slowly above the base, exiting the open doors of the launch bay, rising towards the sky. The sunlight shone dull against the matte hull as the ship rose higher and higher.

"Punch in cruise speed, Manisha," ordered Anara in Ops. They would need to cruise till they cleared the asteroid belt beyond Mars. Navigation at any higher speed would be impossible till that point.

Manisha moved her controls and eased *Antariksh* forward. They would need a few hours to cross the orbit of

Jupiter. They would not take their first *Jump* till well clear of the orbit of Uranus.

The plan was that the first *Jump* would get them to the Oort cloud, after which they would proceed in phases mapping out the space in front of them. Everyone settled down concentrating on their tasks – after all, this was going to be a long journey and they would not be home for at least two years. They were finally on the way to Proxima Centauri.

ANTARIKSH RETURNS, 3.5 LY

*A*ntariksh was cruising back on course to Proxima. Over the past four weeks, the crew had worked hard to learn the new capabilities of the ship while trying to fix radiation leaks. There was a bit of routine back in their work, but vigilance was still high with at least two officers, preferably three, always present in Ops. The cocoon in Ops had also been expanded to hold two people, thus reducing the risk of being caught off-guard even during the *Jump*.

Anara had instituted regular drills for everyone on board beyond what was planned and practiced earlier. Now the drills were focused on responding to attacks, weapons training, evasive actions, target practice and cutting down reaction time at *Jump* terminals. Not being a military crew, some of these were new for many members, but between Rawat and Ryan, the crew was becoming reasonably proficient.

Anara was pleased with how hard her crew was working, but she remained worried. How should she respond if they met the alien ship again? Should she attack first and show her intent of not being cowed down or should she try communicating again? She was spending most of her time analysing footage and data from the last encounter. They'd collected a huge amount of information but even with help from Narada, she was no closer to solving the dilemma in her mind.

She was only able to latch on to one or two inputs; one being the markings on the hull of the alien ship and the other the time lapse between the detection of the increase in heat signature from the ship and the time it had fired the beam. The delay could give them a brief amount of time that could be used to evade the beams. This data was programmed into the autopilot allowing the ship to choose a safe course and dodge the lasers during the battle if the heat signature reached similar levels.

She had reviewed all the signal protocols designed for contact as well as the sequence that had been used. She could not think of any changes to make and decided that SOS was still the best identifier. The aliens may not know what it stood for, but it would clearly identify that *Antariksh* was from Earth, if they understood that *Antariksh* was from Earth. But did they?

She was, however, very clear that the nuclear weapons would not be used on other living beings, whatever the provocation. She would probably have to live with a few deaths on her head if the aliens attacked with even more powerful weapons, but not if the deaths were caused by weapons so destructive, they should have never been invented.

She was also surprised by how easily she had slipped back into thinking like a military commander. She understood why military personnel trained so hard to respond fast and furious. War did not reward the losers. She was still committed to peace, but she was ready to make the choice if required.

Today, as she sat in the cafeteria, she was happy to see her shipmates relaxing around her. There was something about preparation that increased confidence, which in turn reduced stress. The danger was not over, but the crew was ready for the next encounter.

"May I join you, Captain?" Ryan interrupted her thoughts.

"Sure, Commander," she replied, looking up at him. Ryan had also changed over the last few weeks. He was more settled in his role of the second-in-command and had started countering her with his views and own brand of leadership. Their mutual respect had only increased because of this change. His measured response during and after the incident had earned him the admiration of everyone on board.

"Still eating alone, I see, Captain? You should mix with your crew, you know. Try to get to know them better," he observed, as he sat down.

"That's what you're here for, Ryan," she smiled. "Besides, I've been taught there has to be a certain distance between a commander and her crew, lest she starts focusing more on them than her mission."

"You have an exemplary crew, Captain and many of them have joined up to follow you. You personally. It is lonely at the top and it wouldn't hurt if you spent some time with them."

"You won't stop pushing this case, would you Ryan? I'll think about it."

"Great. Let me get something to eat and then I'll be right back with another dose of Ryan's *gyaan*. I mean snippets from my vast intellect." He had picked up a good smattering of the Hindi language during his time in India. "Can I get you anything?"

"No, thank you. I've just finished."

As Ryan moved off, she thought about what he'd said and decided it wouldn't hurt to get to know her crew-members. In all her previous missions, she'd led much smaller teams where she'd been comfortable with close relationships. She realized that no other space-faring captain had led such a huge crew for such an extended mission. This was her chance to set the path for future captains to follow.

Ryan returned with his food.

"How's the lunch today?" asked Anara.

"Not much different from yesterday. But, all said, this is much better than what I'd expected when I joined up."

"I know, right? In our earlier missions, I could only dream of eating off a plate. Then our food came in tubes!"

She paused while Ryan forked a few mouthfuls and sat there chewing silently, watching him intently. He had not joined her without a genuine reason.

"You don't agree with my decision, do you? To continue with nuclear weapons on board?"

"I was wondering when you would bring that up again. I'm sure you would have thought this over, Captain," he replied.

"That is not what I asked, Ryan."

He smiled not looking up at her. "You know, my country once had the largest collection of nuclear weapons on the planet. We were also the first and only country to have used them in battle. The destruction it caused is well documented. It did end a war, but at what cost? Today I am part of a team that has brought the same weapons far beyond Earth. Does that make me any less guilty than the people who placed them on board this ship? Honestly, I'm not happy about this, Captain, but I'll go with your decision. However, I implore you to find a way to deactivate them so that you don't get tempted to use these bombs."

Anara was afraid he'd say this. She'd struggled earlier and now she was questioning her stance once again. Could she live with herself if any weapons on board the ship were used to kill living beings? Till now she had been looking at the lasers in an abstract manner. Something like a gun kept around the house for protection, the owner never really meaning to use it. But if she really had to make a choice: would she or not?

"That's the bitter truth, Ryan. We'll be responsible if these are used, whether we like it or not. Deactivating is a possibility, but as long as they remain on board, the danger is still there."

Both sat silent for some time while Ryan ate his food, ruminating on the state of affairs.

"I promise I'll think some more on this, but I doubt I'll change my mind again," Anara said, finally breaking the silence.

Ryan nodded as he sipped the juice. "It's your decision and you know I'll support it whatever happens. I think I can speak for the crew as well. I see a renewed sense of purpose and less fear. I just wish things had turned out differently."

"How did we land up here, Ryan? We were supposed to be explorers, not soldiers. I never thought the first people we met would attack us."

"Just goes to show, alien nature may not be much different from us humans. They carry the same fear of the unknown and possibly a hatred of anyone who is different. We'll need to be extremely careful. Bravery today has acquired a whole new meaning. No human has faced a more daunting task, fifty-five souls alone in space with an unknown enemy openly threatening them. It was better in the trenches in South America – at least you knew the enemy, even if you could not always see them."

"Hmm. I think that is enough musings for now. We should be getting back to work before the crew starts thinking that the two of us are having second thoughts."

NEAR THE TRI-STARS 3.8 LY

Antariksh was back again. This time they had managed to reach closer to the Proxima Centauri star system without being molested. The small brown dwarf, not visible from Earth, could now be seen with naked eyes, the brightest star in the sky. Detailed scans were being carried out continuously mapping the route forward. They would proceed more at sub-light speeds from this moment.

"Steady as it goes, Manisha," said the Captain. "Anything on the scans yet, Ryan?"

"No, though we are limited to the visible area only. There are some asteroids and smaller planetesimals along our route. All mapped and ready. Astrometry and planet studies are being continuously fed. There is nothing to be concerned about."

"It is surprising that they intercepted us earlier at that distance and are now hiding away. I would have expected a massive welcoming party," observed Anara.

"My views exactly, Captain. Not sure what's going on. My weapons systems are primed and manned. They are getting the same feed as Ops, but the controls will be released only by me," said Major Rawat.

Unlike the last time, being better prepared gave them a sense of confidence, though there was still an undercurrent of tension on the ship.

"Let's drop speed by 25% as we approach. It should give us a bit more time to respond," Anara ordered.

Manisha manipulated the controls and reduced speed. The ship continued to move forward.

The calmness in Ops was shattered as the proximity alarm blared. "Contact!" shouted Ryan, "Bearing 272. Same mass and type as M2575," he said, referring to the designation for the alien ship they'd encountered earlier.

"Sound the ship wide alert, Manisha," Anara ordered as everyone around the bridge started his or her own analysis of the new entity. The alert alarm sounded throughout the ship and people moved rapidly to their respective stations, sending their status to Manisha who received acknowledgements on her screen. In the meantime, Ryan had a display of the location and speed of the object moving towards them.

"All stop," ordered Anara, "let them come to us this time. We will wait here. Major, what is the status of the guns?"

"Primed and ready, Captain, but the safety is on. There will be no accidental shooting."

"Ok, people. Stay sharp; let's see what happens. Manisha, how long before they reach us?"

"Five minutes at current speed."

"Commander, could we have detected them earlier?"

"I don't think so. We've been probing continuously. I think it might've been behind one of the asteroids and moved at high speed to intercept us. I'm putting the visuals on display now."

A familiar sight came up on the display, the same shape and diffused lighting. The holo changed to show relative positions of the two ships and the star system.

"Any idea if it's the same ship or a different one?" asked Anara.

"It is still too far away to make out, Captain. The hull configuration is similar, but I can't make out any markings," replied Ryan.

The Ops crew strapped on their seat safety harnesses to avoid a repeat of the last time and waited for the approaching ship. All eyes were on the holo as the distance between them decreased rapidly until it was less than a hundred kilometres away. Then the other ship stopped moving forward and instead turned sideways. It carried out two sweeps in front of *Antariksh* as if evaluating why the Earth ship had come back. The markings on the vessel were clearly visible now.

"It's not the same ship, going by the markings," observed Ryan.

"Noted," said Anara. "What the hell are they trying to do this time?" she asked no one in particular.

The other ship again came face to face with *Antariksh* and came to a dead stop. Expectation and tension built up on *Antariksh* once again.

Suddenly two bright white lights came on at the front of the alien ship.

"Steady everyone, steady," said Anara as everyone on the bridge started at this sudden change. "Fire now!"

The Major let loose a burst from their new laser cannon as they had planned earlier. A bright bolt of blue shot out and passed a few kilometres to the right of the enemy vessel. They had started thinking of the aliens as the enemy now.

For a moment, there was no response, then the ship made a complete U-turn and scooted back at high speed from where it came from.

The holo traced the ship's path as it went back into the star system and hid from their view behind an asteroid field. The fix on the position gave her confidence that they would not be caught off-guard again. Anara had achieved exactly what she had planned to, namely to plant an element of fear in the enemy's mind. Play the same games that had been played on *Antariksh* earlier.

"Good work, people. I think we've given them something to think about. They should realize that this was only a warning shot and that we're not as helpless as we were last time," said Anara. "Major, secure the cannons."

A few rapid instructions and the cannons went back to standby. They were now going to wait and let the enemy make the move. They had enough time on their hands and would wait this out.

***

The hours passed slowly after *Antariksh* had fired the warning shot. The aliens had not made any move and it could be concluded that the ship was still hiding behind the asteroids. Ops remained watchful with radar focused on the last known position of the alien. Additional continuous sweeps were carried out all around *Antariksh*. They had also been able to determine that the lights from the alien had been just that – lights. It might just be possible that the aliens were trying to communicate. But Anara would communicate only when she deemed it fit. The game had changed.

Then, just as Anara was contemplating ordering a rotation of the Ops crew to enable everyone to get some rest, Ryan called out from his station.

"Contact again," he said. "They're emerging from the field and moving towards us." The ship's sensors had recorded the movement almost as soon as the ship had come out from behind the asteroid.

"Sound the alert, Manisha. Be prepared to move rapidly if we get into a fight. Major, guns ready?"

"Affirm," acknowledged Manisha. She'd been losing her concentration while waiting for the last few hours. The new situation was just what she needed to get her adrenaline flowing again.

"Cannons ready," reported Rawat.

The alien ship came down the same path as before but this time it stopped a thousand kilometres from *Antariksh's* position. Again, the two lights came on, but this time the distance dimmed their impact. Anara and her crew waited for the next move.

The lights changed and started flashing in unison – three long, three short and three longs: SOS.

The bridge crew cheered and even Anara permitted herself a smile. It looked like they wanted to talk after all.

"Let's reply back, Ryan, and see if we can start communicating."

COMMUNICATIONS

The two ships faced each other in empty space. The first exchange of signals had been successful and now each seemed to wait for the other to make the next move.

"Madhavan, let's go to the next stage and transmit signal 1 on EM. Cycle through the frequency band," ordered Anara.

"Wilco," answered Madhavan and entered the necessary commands. The display showed the signals being transmitted and their frequency. It would take some time for them to cycle through the determined spectrum.

"No response," reported Ryan after monitoring the listening post.

"Do you mean they are not responding or that we are not able to read their signal? Any indication they're receiving us at all?"

"Not sure. We're transmitting across a broad beam, so no reason they shouldn't be able to receive us. I'll boost the signal," Madhavan said.

"Ryan, can you scan for increased EM emissions from their ship?" It could be that the two ships did not have compatible receivers or maybe the aliens were using a different technology.

Ryan focused his receivers to scan for all EM directed towards their ship. The computer automatically filtered out background radio waves. He started looking for spikes across various frequencies.

"There are three frequencies showing a spike." Ryan showed them on the main display. Data rapidly scrolled across the screen. "Isolating frequency 3."

"Signal boosted 50%. Matching transmission to frequency 3." Madhavan shifted his transmission to the same frequency.

This seemed like an exercise in iterations till the two ships learned each other's capabilities.

"Still transmitting ones and zeros," Madhavan reported.

"There is some response, I'm sure, but I don't know what it means. Matching with the earlier responses received on Earth." There was a short pause while the computer rapidly executed the command. The output came up on the display as a long line of binary data. "It looks like we are getting somewhere. These are also zeroes and ones."

"Good work. Let's go a bit more complex and send a 'Hello' in binary."

The transmission display changed to show the new signal. The incoming also changed almost immediately to the same digits.

"That's it. We have a working link," observed Anara smiling. "Hand transmission over to my pad." She rapidly entered a series of predetermined phrases indicating her origin, location and peaceful intentions. She had no clue if the beings on the other ship even understood Standard English or if they were merely mirroring whatever they received. Even though it had been decided that English was the language to be used, the Earth ship was at a disadvantage. The aliens may have picked up Earth's common language, but she did not have an idea what their language was. She just had to plod on and hope for the best.

A new set of long strings of binaries appeared on the display and its translation to English appeared next to it.

"What the..." remarked Madhavan. "These are instructions on tuning our transceivers so that we can make video contact. Video contact? We want to do that, right?"

"Can you make the adjustments?" asked Anara.

"This will take some time. A few hours at least. Our systems seem to be broadly compatible – after all the principles of physics and mathematics are universal. But I'll have to set up a parallel set of transceivers or else our primary systems might get affected. I'll also need put in place a second computing node isolated from our primary network in case they try something funny." His computer system had enough checks and balances, but why should he take unnecessary risks?

"Get on with it, then. Ryan will help you. Keep me informed. Major, take over the communication station. Transmit 'Please wait while we make changes to our systems' and let's hope they understand. Manisha, keep an eye on their power outputs just in case."

A new stream of data appeared on the display to show the reply. It said 'OK'.

Anara smiled and shook her head. Either this was a very good attempt by the aliens to understand English or they knew more than enough about Earth. She hoped this was not another way of luring them into complacency. For now, it was back to waiting. In the meantime, the rest of her team would continue to investigate the alien ship and understand its structure.

"Any inputs on the design, Major?"

Rawat was keeping an eye on the feed from *Antariksh's* computer and visual system. "I've been plotting the data collected so far. It's been visual and passive only. I've avoided more intrusive gamma, X-ray and other scans. The ship's volume seems to be at least three-fourths of ours. The same would be the estimate on its weight but we don't know what material it is made from. Negative on their method of propulsion as well. However, there is some radioactive decay in their wake so I would assume that their core power source is atomic or anti-matter based, like ours."

"That's interesting. Go on."

"We have the velocity chart from the two runs they've made, and their ship seems somewhat more manoeuvrable than ours, but I cannot establish their max speed or if they have FTL capability. I just don't have enough data," Rawat finished.

"That is good enough for now. Continue with the analysis and let's get some more conclusions. Do you have any idea if there are people aboard or is it automated?"

"Again, I've no idea, Captain. Would you like me to try the more aggressive scans?" asked Rawat.

"No," said Anara as she mulled it over. "I don't want to do anything that may seem provocative. If they have nuclear power, then they should be able to recognize the radiation we send toward them. Until we know more, I cannot risk exposing them to radiation. Passive only. Manisha, take a dump of the transmissions and data logs on the ship and transmit to Earth," instructed Anara and settled back in her seat.

***

Ryan and Madhavan had a team of engineers working on converting the transceivers to the specifications given by the aliens. The two of them stood side by side in engineering looking down at the work in progress.

"Too bad these didn't come with a step-by-step guide," joked Madhavan. "That would've saved us a lot of time."

Their progress, so far, had been good. They had started off by isolating a transceiver set for this particular use. One team worked on creating a separate computer node dedicated to transmissions to the alien vessel, while the second team adjusted the equipment to a specific frequency. After that, the standard converters would let *Antariksh's* displays handle the output. While the changes themselves were not too complex, it took them some time to carry out the modifications and check the calibrations.

"This is it, then," reported Madhavan, once his final engineering modifications were done. "I think this is all in line. We're good to go, boss."

"Noted, but let's carry out some test runs just to be sure. I hope you've added a filter to ensure the system does not get overloaded if the signal is too strong?"

"No stress, I added a filter and an overload protection. Diagnostics are being run now, but I guess we can test it only in the field. The controls have been routed through Ops. I've also connected our bridge cameras to work with the transceiver. That'll allow us to transmit our visuals."

"Okay. Let's grab a quick bite to eat and report to Ops. I think we've earned it. I'll inform the Captain," said Ryan as he sent off a message to Anara.

***

Anara was waiting for them when they reached Ops. A quick huddle was enough to let her know they were good to go.

"That was good work, both of you. Ryan, let's do this," she acknowledged. She was anxious to make the next move after all the waiting.

"Bringing the transceiver online," said Madhavan. "Ready to transmit and receive on your mark."

"Send 'Hello' again, Ryan," Anara commanded, and the proper signal was sent across. The reply came back a few seconds later.

"Yes! My system is working," said Madhavan, his eyes shining. Anara smiled inwardly.

The display showed two screens; the ship's original transceiver and the modified one, both showed the same answer: 'Hello'.

The modified system output changed on the display and it filled up with static.

"What's happening, Madhavan?" asked Anara.

"We're receiving the signal, but the filter is taking some time to relay it. Give it a moment."

The static resolved slowly into a vague silhouette. Anara leaned forward. What did these aliens really look like? Unlike Europa, this was certainly not microscopic alien life. She held her breath.

"Clearing up now."

The image slowly resolved itself and Anara started. She was prepared to come face to face with any type of alien creatures, but surely not for this.

"They're human!" she exclaimed.

THE 'NEW' HUMANS

The crew sat motionless, staring at the figure on the screen. The only sound was the soft beeps from the holo display. A human face on an alien ship? Four light years from home? What was happening? The roller coaster ride refused to end.

There was no mistaking the figure on display – it was human. Sure, the clothing was different, more rustic and plainer, but the figure was clearly a human male, about 20 years old, Anara guessed. The male moved a little to the side and was joined by a female human with blonde hair.

Still no one spoke up. Human beings were the last things they had been expecting to see. The silence dragged on as the two groups stared at each other across the vastness of space.

Anara finally found her voice. "Greetings from Earth. Can you understand me?" She was glad to be speaking English and not having to rely on binary transmissions.

"Yes, I can understand," replied the male, his soft voice hesitating as he seemed to be struggling to find the correct words.

"My name is Captain Anara from the planet Earth. We have come a long way to meet you." She spoke slowly to allow the aliens to understand her. Should she still call them aliens?

"My name is Joe, Captain Anara, and this is Lucy. We are happy to meet you," the male answered, his voice a bit more confident and a small smile breaking the ice.

"Joe and Lucy, Wow! I... we... are very happy to be here but ... I am confused. What are you doing so far away from Earth? How come you're speaking our language? Are you really human?" Anara asked, her voice betraying her confusion.

"Humans? I am not sure, but you look like us. Captain Anara," replied Joe, "but first we need to move away. It is not safe. The 'Others' will notice and return."

"Others? What 'Others'?" asked Anara.

"We will tell later," Lucy interjected. "Trust us. We must go."

"No. I can't trust you blindly. Where are we going? What're you afraid of?"

"We must go, Captain Anara. Now!" Lucy urged her again.

"Captain, another contact! Like the ship in front, but further away. Coming from outside the system," reported Ryan.

"Time to reach us?" asked Anara, muting the communications.

"Thirty minutes at current speed and distance," answered Ryan. "They're headed this way."

"Options, people?" Anara asked, slightly out of breath.

"We can stay and fight, Captain. But my instinct tells me that we should go with Joe here," said Ryan. "We need some answers to who they are and if they are human, then did they manage to get this far away from home. They look trustworthy enough." Was it just him or was the entire crew overwhelmed by finding humans near Alpha Centauri?

"Major?"

"I don't agree. I am intrigued with Joe, but we can defend ourselves if required," replied Rawat. "We know nothing about these people. The ships are the same; this will be another trap for sure. Joe may be trying to get us to a place from where we cannot escape."

"You may be right Ryan, but I will go with Rawat's suggestion. We have a few minutes so let's see what we can learn." She unmuted the conversation. "Joe," she said. "I'm asking you again - where are we going and why?"

On the display, Joe and Lucy exchanged looks. "Captain Anara, please trust us and do not be afraid. We will go to a safe place and we will explain everything once we get there."

"That's not enough for me, Joe. Some time back one of your ships attacked and nearly crippled us. What can you tell me about it? It may not have been you, but someone has the same ship and they are not friendly," she emphasized.

Joe and Lucy looked alarmed at this piece of news. "It was not us, Captain Anara," Lucy replied. She looked at Joe, who nodded in agreement. "We have only this ship. It must be the 'Others'."

This was getting tiresome. "For the last time, who are the 'Others', Lucy?" asked Anara, more firmly this time.

This time it was Joe who answered. "They are the other people – how you say – group. They don't want us to make contact. We are here to bring you to safety. Please trust us," he implored.

"They look genuine," observed Ryan, "and their ship has different markings. Besides, have we not already demonstrated our power and the fact that we are prepared to defend us? This ship ran away a few hours back in the face of our cannons."

"Joe and Lucy, you have seen what our ship can do to attack. I want to show you again," said Anara. She gestured to the Major who let loose another shot from the cannon.

They could see Joe and Lucy wince as the blue bolt passed their ship.

"We do not understand, Captain. Why do you attack us?" Joe screamed as Lucy shook next to him.

"I did not attack you. This was just a warning shot. I want to demonstrate that we are prepared for a fight, whether we like it or not."

"No fight. No fight. We come in peace!" He was begging.

"Who else is on your ship?" Anara asked. "The two of you cannot be flying it alone."

"We have a few people, Captain Anara, you will see. We have no weapons on this ship. We want peace."

Anara looked at her crew who seemed as perplexed as she was. The people on the alien ship seemed genuinely frightened. It was time for her to make her final call.

"Fifteen minutes for the other ship to reach us," reported Ryan. "We must make a decision now!"

She replied. "Okay Joe, we will go with you. Lead the way. Send us the coordinates."

"Coordinates?" Joe looked confused and then he looked down. "Oh, you mean location. I will send now."

"Then let's go. Manisha, follow the ship," ordered Anara. "Joe," she addressed the other ship, "I will be keeping my guns ready. Don't try anything funny!"

"Funny?" again Joe and Lucy looked both bemused and relieved. "Not funny. Peace. Come."

The ship turned around and headed back to where it came from.

"Match speed and course, Manisha," ordered Anara. "Major, hands on the trigger. Ryan, keep an eye on the other ship and scan ahead. Any idea where we are headed?"

"Deeper into the system, Captain, general direction towards the star system. Straight line towards the second planet." answered Ryan.

"Looks like we'll finally see Proxima B," Anara said as *Antariksh* started moving. *If* it was Proxima B. "What have your readings of the planet shown you so far?"

"Not much. I don't have enough data, but visuals indicate limited amounts of water and plant life. Overall, the planet looks desolate with features somewhat like Mars. However, there's an atmosphere and surprisingly the spectra show a mix of gases similar to Earth with somewhat higher levels of noble gases. I can give you more data once we clear the asteroid belt. The Sun is considerably weaker but since the planet is closer to it than the Earth is to our Sun, the temperature range seems to be in the Circumstellar Habitable Zone - not too hot, not too cold. So, it definitely proves that there are more Goldilocks zones than Earth alone."

"Are there any signs of life or civilization?"

"I can't scan for life this far out, Captain, but I've not seen any large artificial structures to indicate a civilization. I can safely conclude that the findings so far are not consistent with a species capable of building and flying the ship in front of us."

"Let's see some visuals on the screen," asked Anara and the image of a brown green planet presented itself. It was a wondrous sight for the crew to see another planet up close – one capable of supporting life. There were a few spots of blue, liquid water as indicated by their sensors, surrounded by green and red, but most of the planet looked barren in a dust brown colour. There were some white caps, possibly of ice or snow, on the two poles.

"I hope you're recording this for posterity, Ryan. It's so beautiful. And to think it's habitable for humans." Anara leaned back in her chair with her eyes fixed on the screen, the planet revolving slowly with a weak sun shining behind it.

PROXIMA B

The two ships headed deep into the system. The sun, Proxima Centauri, was not bright like Earth's own sun, a fact determined long ago by astronomers on Earth. It was a brown dwarf that was much cooler. This impacted the temperature and overall features of Proxima B.

"Anything else on the scanners?" asked Anara.

"No change. The 'Other' ship is not visible. Joe's ship is still heading into the system. We are 5 million kilometres from Proxima B, and we should be reaching it in... 20 minutes," Ryan replied.

"Dr Khan, did you find anything in the database on humans travelling this far? How the hell did these guys get here?"

"I've checked everything, Captain, and I could only find speculations, a few wild rumours and several downright lies. You know there've been many reported sightings of UFOs on Earth over the last two centuries, but none of them were ever validated. Alien abductions were commonly reported in the media but again investigations debunked most of them. Late in 2060, most records were declassified when the '8' decided to move deeper into the search for extra-terrestrial life. But nothing was found in the archives. In short, no. I don't have anything substantial to report."

"Okay. What about the physiological structures of Joe and Lucy?"

"I only have their physical appearances to go with, but everything corresponds to two healthy human beings of Caucasian descent. Without a detailed analysis and DNA samples I will not be able to do anything more," Khan said.

"Hmm ... you must also have seen that they are both about the same age and very young."

"Yes, then there is another thing: where do you think they learned English? They were not fluent, but they were still pretty good," said Ryan.

"And what about the fact that they have names like Joe and Lucy?" Manisha wondered aloud, then realizing she may have interrupted something. "Sorry."

"No need to apologize, Manisha. You're right. Those names look like something people would've picked up from a movie or a book." Anara was worried. If these people indeed knew a few Earth words, then clearly, she and her ship were at a disadvantage. Anyway, now that the next step has been taken, she might as well see it through.

**

The planet was growing larger in their display and Joe's ship was slowing down. Everyone on *Antariksh* was at a view port or a display. The dull brown planet with the specks of blue and green kept growing larger. It looked even more inhospitable and bleak up close, barely capable of supporting life, let alone an advanced civilisation capable of space travel.

"What are the surface conditions like, Manisha?"

"The temperature is ranging from 15 degrees to 35 degrees Celsius. Humidity is 15%, cloud cover minimal, winds 30 to 40 kmph. Nothing remarkable, Captain. It's rocky rather than sandy and precipitation is low. There are a couple of large water bodies, possibly seas, no oceans, a few lakes, which may have fresh water but most of the water seems to be underground. There is some vegetation but not many large trees or forests."

"The temperature looks suitable for human life and there is water. Is the atmospheric gas composition as we'd seen earlier? Is there any animal life?"

"The atmospheric composition is similar to that of the Earth. Thermal and infrared scans do not indicate life on the land this side. The water bodies are empty too."

Joe's ship was descending on a long arc, heading towards the other side of the planet. *Antariksh* followed the same path.

"New readings," reported Ryan as the ship followed the planet's curve. "There's another lake on this side as well as a small settlement."

The blue of the lake and the green of the settlement, though miniscule from this height, were nevertheless clearly visible from orbit against the stark brown of the land around.

Joe's ship started losing altitude and seemed to be preparing for landing.

"Looks like they are getting ready to land," said Ryan.

"Yes, it does. Manisha, prepare *Antariksh* to land too. Heat shields up. Let the crew know that they must get buckled up for atmospheric turbulence," ordered Anara.

Antariksh started its own descent behind Joe's ship. The hull temperature rose steadily as it encountered the atmosphere. The ship's speed started dropping and Manisha deployed the thruster engines to help them land.

The settlement came into focus and they could see three clearings, probably serving as landing pads, a little distance outside its perimeter. Some fields of grain surrounded the pads and they could just make out some human shapes moving around.

"Looks like Joe and Lucy are not the only humans on this planet. Scan for human signatures and biological threats."

"I am reading at least fifty human heat signatures in the settlement, Captain," Manisha reported shortly after.

"I also see multiple bacteria and viruses in the air. Mostly unknown to us. I would recommend EVA suits if we are going out," reported Khan. Extravehicular Activity or EVA suits would provide them a self-contained atmosphere to work in for an extended period while protecting the crew from any harmful organisms.

"Noted. We also need to protect whoever is down there. They will not have our immunity to Earth organisms. What we don't want is to kill the local population with a common cold," said Anara drily.

"There's something else you should see. Fifteen kilometres to the west of the settlement. I'm zooming in now," said Ryan, his hands manipulating the controls.

The object that came into focus spread across tens of acres, its shape immediately recognizable.

"A radio telescope," breathed Ryan. "It's massive. This could've been the one used to send the signals we received back on Earth."

"Keep recording, Ryan. Narada, send data transmission with logs up to this point back to Earth. Also drop a data pod, keeping it on the northern pole of the planet. Push the same information to it. Set it to serve as repeater, storage and beacon. Never know what awaits us."

"Transmission sent. Pod prepared and loaded. Deploying now," reported Narada.

"What are your orders, Captain? Should we land on the planet? We'll be exposed to attacks both from the orbit or ground and taking off will take time, leaving us vulnerable," said Ryan.

"My thoughts exactly. Clearly, we must land if we want to learn anything more. Joe and Lucy are certainly not going to tell us anything more up here. But I hate to lead the whole ship and crew into danger unless it is absolutely necessary."

"A small party then?" asked Rawat. "You, me, Dr Khan, Dr Lian, one member from the science and medical teams as well as a couple of security people?"

"Captain, I strongly suggest that you do not go down there," argued Ryan. "The situation is too dangerous and unpredictable. Besides, you will be on an unknown planet with natural dangers, completely exposed to attack from the enemy ship pursuing us. I strongly suggest you stay aboard *Antariksh* and let me go in your place."

"Do you want to rob me of the greatest moment since humans set foot on Jupiter's moons, Ryan?" Anara asked with a smile. "No. I will be selfish here. I am going down to meet them. Besides, I'll have enough people around me, not counting the humans already on the planet. Let's land this ship."

"Aye, Captain." He gave a mock salute. It was true that this moment required the senior most representative from Earth to make first contact.

Antariksh followed the other ship and landed next to it on one of the pads. They waited for Joe and Lucy to guide them on the next steps. Meanwhile, samplers were deployed to collect specimens from the atmosphere and soil, and Manisha scanned the surroundings for additional threats while mapping the terrain.

"There are two power signatures. Possibly the settlement's power plants. Size and capacity are unknown, located on the far side," she reported.

"Noted. If there are no other threats visible, let's be on our way. Ryan, you're in command in my absence. You will go back into orbit and if the other aliens come back, you'll have to hold them off. In any case, if the ship is in any danger, leave the system immediately. We'll stay with Joe and Lucy and hopefully they'll be able to protect us. You can come pick us up when we're ready. We will stay in constant touch over the intercom. Expect me to check in every hour," ordered Anara as she gestured for the rest of the team to get ready to join her.

"I know we're taking a big risk, Ryan," she continued, looking at the concern on his face, "but we will not find answers if we stay in our ship. We'll take personal weapons and I'll have two of Rawat's heavyweights with me."

"Noted," agreed Ryan with a sigh. She had clearly made up her mind, and they did not have enough time to argue over this. "Best of luck and if I may say, congratulations! We've finally reached our destination!"

ASSESSMENT ON EARTH

Srinivas had been called back to the PM's office. The original members of the cabinet and scientists were assembled again. This time there were no presentations, just questions to be answered. He was not sure if he had all the answers.

"Director," said the PM, "we're eager to hear the progress report from the mission."

"Yes, sir. As I'd indicated in my last report, we don't have a fix on their position beyond Pluto. The mission had progressed quite smoothly till that position. There have been no malfunctions that we can determine, and the crew was last reported to be in good health. The *Jumps* taking them outside the solar system worked as designed and no adverse effects were noted."

"Has there been any other contact with Proxima?" the PM asked.

"No, sir. We have been transmitting continuously for the last two decades and increased the frequency of transmissions in the last five years including the message that our ship is on the way. Again, we have no way of knowing if it has been received. The relevant frequencies are being monitored, but there have been no replies whatsoever."

"What's your theory, Srini?" asked the PM. "Why have they been silent for so long?"

"It is impossible for me to say, sir," he said, shrugging his shoulders. "The time for them to receive our signal and for us to get their reply was more than sufficient. So that is not the constraint. It may well be a political decision if they have a government. Maybe they got cold feet or even experienced a breakdown in their equipment. I'm afraid we just don't have enough information. However, as the ship gets closer to Proxima, we should be able to get some answers."

"This troubles me, Srini. If we assume the political situation has changed, then our ship may well be flying into danger. Anara can't call us for help. We can't provide it, even if we want to. We can't send them a message asking them to take precautions. It is like sending lambs to slaughter," the PM said with worry.

"If I may," said the Defence Minister. "We do have some means on board to allow the ship to defend itself in case of eventualities."

Srinivas raised his eyebrows. How could the minister make such a basic mistake? "I'm sorry, sir, I don't see how," countered Srini. "The laser guns on board are of very low yield. I don't expect them to be really useful in a conflict situation."

"I was not referring to the laser guns, Srini," said Balraj, taking a glance at the PM. "Maybe it is time that we brief Srini, Prime Minister?"

The Prime Minister was silent while he mulled over this request, then he slowly nodded. Srini looked at them, his eyebrows rising higher.

"Brief me on what, sir?"

"There's something you should know, Srini. Do you remember the short interlude when we stopped the construction work on *Antariksh*? Well, we added some features to the ship through the DRDO in secret."

"Features, sir? You mean weapons?" he asked, understanding slowly dawning on him. Why had Pratyush not said anything about this to him?

"Pratyush was under my direct orders not to reveal this, Srini," said the PM as if divining his thoughts.

"You see, Director, I thought it prudent to arm our ship to face any eventualities so far away from home," said the Defence Minister. "I agreed with the assessment of my predecessors, and we have prepared for many years. You will agree that this decision will now come in handy."

"What have you placed on board, sir?" Srini asked, almost afraid of the answer.

"Heavy duty laser cannons and a few thermonuclear devices."

Thermonuclear devices? Oh God! He means nuclear bombs! The Director's heart sank. The ship was already nuclear powered and now the risk was increased because of these bombs.

"Don't worry, Director. These bombs are more of a deterrent than for actual use. I've ensured dual responsibility for arming them. In case of trouble Major Rawat will brief the captain immediately. And if there's no trouble, the bombs will remain hidden and come back to us eventually," said the Defence Minister.

"Will they come back, sir? We've let loose nuclear bombs into deep space in the hands of people who are alone and may be threatened. What happens if they are so consumed with fear that they end up using these bombs? Will it not result in an interstellar war? We have sent weapons of mass destruction into deep space!"

The PM spoke up. "I appreciate what you are saying, Srini, but this was necessary. I am confident that our team will handle this with the respect it requires. Now, on to the other thing," continued the PM, changing track. "Director, we need another ship."

"Another ship, sir?" confused by the change of tracks.

"Yes, Srini. We've demonstrated our capability to travel to interstellar space. Even if *Antariksh* fails to reach Proxima, we should start improving on the original design and construct a bigger, more powerful ship," the PM explained. He got up from his seat and walked across the room. "There are two reasons why we must do this, Srini. One, we need to look beyond the stars closest to us and go further into the cosmos. Two, should *Antariksh* discover something inimical to Earth's interest, we need powerful ships to defend ourselves and, if required, to take the war to the enemy's planet. We could have done this earlier but resources though available were not unlimited."

Though he was deeply disturbed, Srini knew that circumstances were beyond him now. He realized that life as they knew it on Earth had changed again, but he was surprised that the PM, who had always advocated for peace was now talking about war. Maybe the military mind-set of the defence minister had got to him or maybe it was the '8'. He decided to persist a little longer.

"Why are we thinking of war, sir? Nothing so far has indicated a threat to Earth."

"That is quite true, Srini. But over the last few months, as I have waited for news from *Antariksh*, I have drawn strength from the fact that those people have sufficient means to protect themselves. You do not send an explorer into the jungle without a rifle, knowing that there are predators who might harm him, right?" The PM's conviction came through his words. "Anyway, we want you to concentrate on building a ship that is faster, can carry more people, function independently and be able to communicate with Earth whenever required. This is the simple brief available to you," instructed the Minister for Space Exploration.

"Yes sir, I will get on with it," Srini nodded to the people in the room, stood up and stepped out of the conference.

"I want to make it clear, Balraj," said the PM once Srini left the room. "No more nuclear weapons. We need alternatives. We have a proven model of spaceflight that works. I want FTL communication to be your top priority. We will explore space from a position of strength, not to threaten those we meet, but to ensure that we are treated as equals."

"I understand, Prime Minister. I have teams working on that even now. We have an experimental transceiver on board the *Antariksh* too and once we have a working solution, I will come back to you," said the Defence Minister.

THE HUMAN SETTLEMENT

Anara stepped off the ship and walked onto the landing pad. Having spent months in space, the weak sunlight felt good on her face, even though her adaptable EVA suit. The light was softer and somewhat diffused, unlike the sunlight back on Earth. She walked a few steps, turned around and noticed fewer colours than on Earth and the absence of large trees. Her crew followed her one by one, the security officers protecting the entire group.

They all marvelled at the fact they were now in a completely different solar system; on a planet almost unknown to humans. It felt much better than Mars or Jupiter's moons where humans were constrained to remain inside environmental domes.

They all headed slowly towards the other ship. The gravity felt stronger than on Earth and after having been on the ship at 0.9g, their steps felt leaden. Their bodies would need time to adapt. The heads up display in their suits streamed data steadily and the intercom systems chirped with various observations of the team members.

Once they were at a safe distance, *Antariksh* lifted off slowly. Rising steadily, it was soon lost to view, and their only contact would now be through their EVA suits. They had limited supplies of food and water. A drone followed them with the scientific and medical instruments. Joe's ship remained silent on the pad.

Joe and Lucy were waiting near their own ship. A few more humans stood around them. Anara had not noticed if they had come from the ship or the settlement. All of them looked to be of the same age with an equal mix of males and females. The two groups walked towards each other, one in orange survival gear and the other in grey trousers and tunics. Anara's security guys were alert, wary of the other humans. They were carrying one projectile pistol each but were under strict orders from Anara to keep them hidden, and to use them as a last resort only.

"Welcome to HuZryss," greeted Joe, smiling. "This is home. We go to village and then we can talk." His voice was soft again and the small grammatical mistakes somehow made it attractive.

Anara nodded, and the group started to move towards the village, walking along a roughly paved path. The village did not seem to have any particular structure with a motley collection of roughly made houses. It was laid out in a roughly spherical shape. The houses were spartan and plainly finished. The streets were paved but dusty. However, the absence of trees and the colours of plants gave the entire scene a surreal look. Everything seemed to be in grey and black with a few rust colours thrown in. There was very little vegetation within the compound.

They walked towards the centre of the village on what Anara assumed was the main street as it was slightly wider than the other roads. More humans, young, fit and roughly dressed could be seen in small groups, looking at them with wide eyes. *They must be as curious about us as we are about them.* The questions in her mind were coming up fast, but she restrained herself. She felt it odd that they had not met a single true 'alien' so far. "Where are we going,

Joe?" she asked, her voice coming clear through her EVA helmet.

"We go to the hall, Captain Anara. People wait for you," Joe answered, striding ahead of the group, Lucy holding his hands.

As they moved deeper into the village towards a larger building, Anara received a message from Ryan that *Antariksh* was now in orbit directly above their position. They would now maintain an open channel with Ops control so that the senior crew on the ship could follow the proceedings on the surface, ready to jump into action if required.

The building seemed to be some type of communal meeting place. Another bunch of people were waiting outside the hall and excitement was clearly visible on their faces. They were talking animatedly; repeatedly pointing towards Anara and her people in their orange garb.

The new humans all looked the same age, but with a mixed ancestry from an Earth perspective. Anara wondered about this as the noisy chatter died down. The Earth group approached, and they all filed into the hall. Rawat gestured to one of the security people to take up positions outside the doors. Nish stood guard fingering the weapon in his pocket, alert but uneasy to be left alone outside.

The inside of the hall was just as spartan as the rest of the village. There were a few simple benches set in the middle in a circle facing the centre. Anara stood around till Lucy invited them to sit down on the benches in the front while the humans of HuZryss waited. Then one by one everyone settled down, the air thick with anticipation.

"Joe," said Anara, taking the lead, "I find it remarkable that humans have found their way so far from Earth, especially since we have just managed to reach speeds that enable us to travel to another star system. We have trusted you so far. Now we need some answers. Who are you?"

"Captain Anara," there was sadness in his voice as Joe answered, "we are the people who are not wanted."

"What do you mean 'not wanted'?" Anara was intrigued. "I don't understand."

"Joe cannot tell where we come from because he does not know. None of us knows," another person interjected. "My name is Jim."

"Jim," Anara repeated, trying to make sense of what she had just heard. Another common monosyllabic name! What the hell was this?

"We are fifty people here. The 'Guardians' brought us here some time ago to save us from the 'Others'. This is where we live now," said Joe.

"Brought you from where? Who are these Guardians? Who taught you English, for God's sake?" exclaimed Anara.

"I will tell you our story, Captain Anara," said Lucy. "I cannot tell where we come from. I do not know. We were small. I remember when we were on a different planet. The Guardians took care of us. There was a building we all lived in. It was a good time."

"Were there more of you?"

"No, always this many from what I remember," answered Lucy, looking at the others as if confirming she had understood the question. Her companions nodded back.

"We were there for twenty or thirty rounds. The Guardians always were with us. They teach us things, take care of us, and give food. We did not go out of building. We only knew the Guardians."

"What do these Guardians look like, Lucy? Like you and me or different?"

"Oh. Uh… I don't know how to explain. They are large," she stood on her tiptoes and raised her hand above her head, to indicate the Guardian's height. *That would be just above six feet,* thought Anara.

"Go on," Anara encouraged, hanging on to every word. This was better than any mystery thriller she had ever read, despite the broken English being used by the group.

"They are dark in colour, how you say, like that," said Lucy pointing to the colour of the equipment container carried by the doctor. *Dark green.* "But more hands." Lucy held up four fingers. "And they walk like us and on the ground."

"You don't have any pictures of them, by any chance?"

"Pictures? No. I do not."

"And the Others? They are of the same species or different?"

"Same. But they are… angry with us. They cause much trouble."

"How so?"

"When we were small, we were not allowed to go out. The building was large, and the Guardians took care. Then one day many people came into the building. They carried… weapons, yes? They broke things and tried to hurt the Guardians and us. But the soldiers came and saved us. They took us out of the building and into a camp. That was the first time we saw the city. It was very big, very beautiful. We stayed at camp for many days. Then one day two big ships came – like the ship outside. All of us and a few Guardians were brought here on the ships."

"First time on ship for us," chimed in Jim. "We go into the sky and near the stars. They brought us here to HuZryss."

"This village was ready for us, they said," said Lucy taking over the narrative, "for our protection from the 'Others'. Every few weeks we get some food and other supplies, but now the Guardians don't come many times. We are alone. No one wants us."

"How did you learn to speak English?" was Anara's next question.

"When we came here first, there were many teachers to tell us how to live on HuZryss. They showed us how to use the machines and grow plants for food. Then they left, coming sometimes to check and bring some supplies. One time many Guardians came. They said someone is coming from the stars to meet us from our home. We did not understand, and they said it will become clear. They said we needed to learn a new language to talk to you, and how to fly the ship. For many days they stay here and taught till all of us learned the language," Lucy added.

"And that is how you could fly the ship to come and meet us," said Anara. "Tell me, Lucy, all of you seem to be the same age. Where are the children and the old people in your community?"

"Children?" repeated Lucy as Joe bent over and whispered in her ear. "We have no children, Captain, or old people, only us."

"And where do the Guardians live?" What planet?"

"It is some days from here. This is HuZryss, that is KifrWyss," she answered.

"KifrWyss?" Anara rolled the name on her tongue. *Like a hiss. Reptilians?* "Is that the name of the Guardian's planet?" asked Anara.

"Yes. It is far away."

"What about the radio telescope nearby? Who set it up and who operates it?"

"What is a radio telescope?" asked Lucy while her people looked equally mystified.

"That large structure of metal close to your village," clarified Anara.

"Oh, you mean Post," she answered, shrugging her shoulders. "It was here when we landed. It is forbidden for us to go there. We do not know what its purpose is."

Her answers were raising more questions in Anara's mind. She was sensing that these humans had somehow been brought to the Guardians planet and were certainly not indigenous to KifrWyss. That would explain the need to keep them in seclusion for their safety. She would have to meet with the Guardians if she wanted to find out more. In the meantime, there were a few things that had to be done. These humans did not seem to have the answers she was seeking.

"We also need something from you, Captain," asked Joe a little hesitatingly. "Where are you from? You look like us, only a little different. Are we ... related?"

"We are from a planet called Earth, which is from a solar system many light years from HuZryss," she answered. She was not sure whether these humans would understand her references to light years, distances and space travel. "We received a signal from this place many years ago and we have come to investigate. There are more than eight billion people like you on Earth and to tell you the truth we never ever expected to find humans here."

She paused while she looked around the room. These people looked more confused and intrigued than frightened. *God knows what they had been going through.* Maybe the rumours about alien abduction were true after all, but she still did not believe that the answer could be so simple. There were too many variables.

"Lucy, before I tell you more, do you mind if Dr Khan here takes some samples of you and your people's blood and tissue to run some tests? That will help us find out more about you. I promise it will not hurt."

"Samples?" a murmur ran through the group. Joe gestured for his people to join him in a corner. They all huddled together, seemingly arguing on Anara's request. This time they were speaking in a strange tongue. Anara made a mental note to ask them about their language database so that she could build a translation program with her computer.

Khan moved to sit beside Anara. "Captain, I carried out some basic analysis while you were talking. These people have all the characteristics of the human race. Of course, it's not possible to be certain till after the tests. But I am not sure if that tells us anything about their origin? How did they land up on a planet, light years from Earth?"

"One thing at a time, Doc. It's beginning to look like we are in the middle of a situation bigger than anything we anticipated. Let me contact the ship while we wait. I need Madhavan to do some digging."

NEW CONFIGURATIONS

"**A**ffirm that you want me to scan the radio telescope on the planet below and find out how it works and if we can use it to send a signal back to Earth," said Madhavan.

"What is happening down there, Captain?" asked Ryan. "I heard the discussions, but I can't make sense of it. Who are these people?" He seemed to be echoing Khan.

"I'm sending more data to the ship that has been collected here over the last few hours, Commander. Go through it and transmit a copy to Earth. To answer your question, we still don't know who these people are. If they allow us some blood samples, it may help us find out. Till then you and I are in the same boat, but there has been some progress. Dr Khan is just getting started on getting samples. He wants to start off with a genetic analysis. He'll connect with you once the samples are ready."

"Understood."

"What about the other ship, Ryan? Any idea where it is?"

"Negative. We've not seen any trace of them. We have been scanning constantly. Of course, if it is hidden behind an asteroid or a moon or even on the other side of the planet, we may not see it."

"That is a problem we need to live with. Keep the crew on alert to respond if anything changes. Anything else?"

"Yes, I deep scanned Joe's ship while it is parked below. It seems empty, but I am building up data on its structure and design. Maybe we can learn something that will give us an advantage."

"Good thinking, Ryan. I seem to have missed that. Can you also do a deep scan for biological readings on the planet surface? It might be a good idea to drop some probes into the water bodies to take some readings."

"On it, Captain. I have three probes prepared for launch."

"I'll contact you soon on schedule. Anara out."

***

"Okay, people," Ryan ordered. "You heard what she said. Let's get to work. Manisha, you keep on the trace for the other ship. I'll get someone to relieve you in a couple of hours. Sandy, you are on the probes. Let's go over the three areas that we've selected. Collect all data and report back to me in four hours. Madhavan, you're on the telescope."

Everyone in Ops got busy while Madhavan and Ryan moved over to the science station. Madhavan focused a camera on the radio telescope and received images across the spectrum.

"There is a very low heat signature; looks like it's powered down. Getting readings on the size and scale. Narada, get a scale diagram drawn up and get me some numbers on the power pack on this system." He still did not trust the AI, but Narada could at least be trusted with data analysis.

"We also need to see if it's pointing towards Earth and if it transmits in the narrow or broad band. Get one of your computer experts up here, Madhavan. Let's see if we can break into its control system," instructed Ryan.

"While we are at it, why don't we see if it's possible to tap into the alien ship's system too? Worst-case scenario we learn how the system is set up."

Ryan nodded slowly. "Yes, but get different teams on the two systems, they can compare notes later. We need answers fast and the more people working on this the better."

Leaving Madhavan to get his people set up, he moved across to Manisha's station.

"Well, Lieutenant, I hope you are tracking the surface team. How many people are there on the surface with them?"

"Fifty, Commander, apart from our crew. They are all in the central structure."

"And still nothing on the other ship?" he asked, and Manisha shook her head. "Keep scanning, and while you're at it, look for some means to see behind the planet. We need to monitor the dark side too in case the enemy tries to sneak up on us from that side." Then he got an idea. "Tell me, Madhavan," he called across to the engineer, "our data pods - they have both send and receive capability, right?"

"Of course, boss," answered Madhavan, intrigued.

"And they can transmit over a large frequency range?"

"Well, there is a limitation because of their size, but yep, the range is fairly good."

"So, if we program a few pods to send out scanning beams continuously, and in turn relay the results to the ship, we can effectively extend the range of our own sensors?"

Madhavan suddenly understood. "Yes, and if we link all of them together, we can actually extend both the width and depth of the search. Want me to get this done?"

"Absolutely. Feed all the data to Manisha. Narada, set the system up for correlating all findings and displaying them on holo. Get a view of the surrounding system; ask the astrometric team to send across their data too. I need to go through the recordings sent by the captain and see what they have learnt."

"I have already scanned the recording, Commander. It's set up to play on your station. There is a regular reference to someone called the 'Guardians' who seem to be from another system. I have asked astrometric to send across a star map so that we can check that out."

"Good work, Narada. We have a lot of stuff to cover."

Ryan moved across to his station and started going through the recordings. He zoomed on specific areas of the village and ran the readings through multiple filters to get a detailed layout view. He assigned individual identifiers to each life signature and mapped them onto a database. He needed to build a full-scale understanding of the encampment below by the time the captain came back.

FRESH DISCOVERIES

The atmosphere in the communal hall was more relaxed now that the HuZryss people had come to an agreement to share all they knew with the humans from Earth. Khan and Lian had moved among the people and started drawing samples and cataloguing them. Base data was sent to the ship for analysis and the results were coming back. One team on the ship and another on the surface would be working together to tabulate the results.

The two sets of people had mixed up within themselves and there was a lot of chatter in the room. Day and night on this planet were nothing like on Earth because of the shorter rotation period of the planet. Over a period, some inhabitants had wandered off, presumably to attend to their routine tasks. Anara and her crew had already gone through two day-and-night cycles.

Anara went outside to join the science and medical teams inside the environment shelter that was set up next to the community hall. This was now the base of their operations on the surface where the team members could work, eat and sleep without their EVA suits.

As she entered, she saw some of her crew catching some shut-eye while Khan was huddled over the display, which was spewing copious amounts of data with charts and graphs. She approached him, taking off her helmet and allowing her dark hair to fall free. It felt good to get out the confines of the suit. Dr Khan's demeanour betrayed his tiredness, but his eyes were bright.

"You're just in time, Captain," he said, "I have the first results of the genetic and physiological analysis we had carried out."

"And…?" Anara prompted.

"There's no doubt about it. These people are as human as we are. At least now we can set that conjecture to rest and move ahead. Also, I can confidently state that they're not a result of genetic manipulation. There is no evidence of commonality in their genes. In fact, they are as diverse as I would like them to be if I was planning to colonise a planet. The gene pool is too small for viable propagation. And their age, as far as I can determine, is similar almost to the day."

"Really? You're saying they share the same birthday? So, we have a set of people who were most likely conceived naturally or at worst through an artificial process, and brought to life, would that be correct?"

"Yes, and I've found no evidence of any Earth-based disease having affected them in their lifetime. Except for the genetic markers for hereditary diseases they're healthy. That would indicate, in all likelihood, that they have been raised in an environment alien to Earth or under absolutely sterile conditions."

"Like HuZryss, KifrWyss or…"

"… or a lab," Khan finished her sentence.

"This is huge, Doc! It would seem the HuZryss have been truthful with us so far, even though I can't imagine them living without parents or any other human contact for so long."

"That brings me to another issue, Captain," said Dr Khan. "Lucy is pregnant."

"Oh! That's a bit of a surprise. I did not expect these people to even know about conception. Does she know?"

"Biological urges cannot be contained, Captain, can they? It's still early, so she might've missed the signs even if she knew what they were. I will speak to her, with your permission. And before you ask, none of the other females are pregnant."

"Hold on to that for a while. We mustn't break their life-cycle without knowing more about the background and their Guardians. In fact, I don't want this information passed beyond you and me for the moment till we decide how to act on it. I'm sure you've already determined who the father is? I trust this is a natural pregnancy?"

"Yes, it is, as far as I can tell, and no, I do not know who the father is. I thought it would be a breach of privacy though it would be easy to determine since I have everyone's DNA samples. And I understand the need for secrecy. I'll move the records to my confidential file."

Anara nodded and went out of the tent, putting on her helmet and zipping up her EVA suit, her mind now working overtime. She wasn't sure how to handle the news of this pregnancy. What had been proven again was that nature always finds a way to propagate a species. These guys had no clue about human procreation, she guessed, but when had that stopped life?

As she stepped out, she saw a crewmember working on the soil samples and walked over to find out what she had discovered.

The scientist looked up as Anara approached and picked up her pad lying next to her on the ground.

"What have you found, Katina?"

"Quite a bit, Captain. I was waiting for Dr Lian to get up before we shared the report with you," answered Katina. She had been seconded from the Russian Academy of Sciences to the mission and though most of her work in geology was carried out in the background, she was revelling in building an understanding of an alien world.

"You can give me a gist and then we can cover it in more detail with Lian."

"Yes, ma'am. The planet has not undergone any large-scale ecological manipulations that I can determine, at least in the vicinity of our location. This water body is natural, and I had asked the team on *Antariksh* to carry out a geological survey. They have determined that the water is from underground sources. I can't find much evidence of rainfall or precipitation, so it's quite possible that the moisture is locked up below the surface."

"So, the water occurs naturally and yet there is no evidence of life beyond bacteria and viruses and there's very limited plant life. Looks almost barren, but still, after Earth, this'll be the third place where life has developed, if we assume that there is another planet where the Guardians come from."

"Yes, Captain. The minerals in the soil, volcanic activity and air composition are all very similar to Earth and the environment is in the 'Goldilocks' zone where life can develop naturally. However, I will not be able to say for sure if that was indeed the case for HuZryss. A lot more research would be required by the astrobiologists."

"Of course, Katina. What else are you looking for?"

"First, Dr Lian has asked me to complete the analysis of the local area and then expand the search. She has requisitioned some drones to collect samples some distance away from here. Those samples will be sent directly to the ship. We're also collecting samples from the depths of the water bodies and drilling to see if we can reach the underground water tables. All this will help us build a geological picture of the planet."

"Keep at it then. I will talk to you again soon," Anara said and stood up. She pondered on what to do next.

Geology was important, but it did not hold her interest. She was smart enough to leave the details to those who were good at it.

Knowing the history of the planet's development would give them an understanding of its suitability for future colonisation, provided the Guardians approved, she thought. This question of who 'owned' the planet and its resources was for the legal minds back on Earth to decide. As far as Earth's solar system was concerned, international convention and treaties clearly applied, though not always complied with. These treaties specified that the planets, moons and other bodies were community resources. How the Guardians would view those conventions would be interesting. If the nations on Earth were fierce in protecting their territory, why not the Guardians or whoever else laying a claim on this planet?

She decided to go back to the hall to see what was developing. It was time to tell the HuZryss where they came from. However, the 'new humans' themselves still had very limited information to share. The Guardians, on the other hand, would be able to provide all the answers she was looking for. She was now willing to even reach out to the Others if only it would help.

The major joined her as she walked back. "This is a very indefensible location, and these people don't seem to have any weapons at all. Their guardians have left them helpless," he remarked.

"Weapons, Major? What do you need weapons for on a deserted planet?"

"Ah yes, it's supposedly deserted, but we have come here, right? What if we were a vicious space faring species out to conquer this world?"

"You are being overly dramatic, Major," Anara said with a smile. "Anyway, I might as well get all my reports for the day. What have you discovered?"

"Nothing special. They have no defensive or offensive capabilities. Their ship's weapons seem to be a watered-down version of the one that attacked us and that is the only weapon on this whole damn planet. If they were so scared of the Others, I would have expected them to be better armed. There isn't a projectile rifle or even a bow and arrow. I guess since there are no animals, they don't know how to hunt either."

"Maybe that is exactly what the Guardians wanted, Major. Leaving these people alone like this may all be part of a larger plan, have you thought about that?" said Anara. "Now I want you to do something. We have only three combatants in our group, you and your two guards. The three of you need to split up so that we can react better in case of an emergency. Having all three of you in one place sort of defeats the whole purpose of having security. We need a bit of stealth, and honestly, I do not see any threat from these humans of HuZryss. Our threat will be from the Others or even from the Guardians."

"Hmm. Do you expect them to come back, Captain?"

"I expect both of them to come sooner or later, Major," said Anara drily. "The Guardians are undoubtedly on their way, based on what Joe has told us and I am sure the Others are just biding their time, somewhere close within the system."

They had reached the hall, and she stepped past the guard leaving the major to have a word with him. The hall was now half empty, though the designated leaders still sat together with a small congregation in the centre of the room. She walked towards the group while waving Khan over to join her.

THE 'OTHERS' ARRIVE

"What do you have, Narada? Get it on holo immediately," Ryan ordered over the din of the alarms. Some of his key people had been sent off to rest, but he expected they would be running to their stations. He was glad about the drills in the recent weeks, which had at least ensured the personnel would react fast. He was relieved to see Manisha enter Ops and take her position. He needed her expertise in case they had to run or land in a hurry. He had sent Madhavan to the power plant and the major's deputy, Lieutenant Keisham, was at the security station.

"We have a single contact, Commander. The distance is 2 million kilometres. It's closing in at cruising speed. Vessel size and configuration are the same as the M2575 we had encountered earlier. Data transferred to holo," reported Narada. A new red symbol for M2982 appeared on the holo with distance, velocity and vector readings showing below it.

"Manisha, send an urgent message to the captain - the enemy is back. We're going to try to keep it away from the planet while awaiting your instructions. Narada, program and send data to the pod above the pole."

"Message sent, priority 1. No response yet."

"Lieutenant Keisham," he addressed the security officer, "get the guns prepped and ready to fire on my command. Madhavan, get the power up to full capacity. We'll need it pretty soon."

"Yes, sir," the Lieutenant and Madhavan acknowledged simultaneously. The Lieutenant had trained with the Major over the last few weeks and they had practiced getting the weapons operational within ten seconds.

As the preparations were completed, everyone's attention was drawn back to the red symbol on the holo, which was inexorably drawing nearer. At ten thousand kilometres out its speed decreased to a hundred kilometres per second.

"Ready for action, people? Manisha, program evasive action if required and transfer control to Narada," Ryan ordered. The AI would be able to respond much faster in this situation.

Manisha's hands moved over the pad inputting commands while her eyes flitted between the holo, her display and the image on the view screen. She had handed over controls but could take them back immediately if instructed.

This time the enemy did not even wait to get close. It made its intentions clear while still many kilometres out, as a red flash of a laser lanced towards *Antariksh*. The ship lurched to one side. This split-second timing still resulted in the laser beam connecting briefly with the hull before being deflected. More alarms sounded across Ops as damage data from sensors flowed onto the screens.

"Time to fight! Narada, all damage data should be available only to engineering for now. Keep the screens in Ops clear!"

Ryan decided to hold fire as his guns would not load fast enough for him to manoeuvre and shoot at the same time. He needed to get some distance between the two ships.

"Narada, new heading. Keep us pointed towards the enemy," he ordered. He needed his line of sight clear.

A second red flash came from the enemy ship and again *Antariksh* lurched as Narada moved them aside.

"Lieutenant, fire one shot. Full power," Ryan ordered. The games were now on.

Blue laser beams shot out of *Antariksh,* but the enemy ship managed to dodge them.

"They seem to be prepared and that ship looks more manoeuvrable," observed Ryan, more to himself than to the others. "Load projectile cannons. Fire one. Fire two!" Even though the range of the projectiles was limited, Ryan hoped that the explosions would distract the Others. He would need to economize the projectile cannons because he had a very limited supply, but maybe the enemy would not be expecting high explosive shells from *Antariksh.*

"One and two fired," reported the Lieutenant, as two HEs were launched. Both travelled a short distance and exploded several kilometres in front of the ship.

There was no impact on the incoming ship, not that Ryan had expected it to be. This was just another show of force.

The third volley from the enemy ship moved across space towards them and once more they managed to dodge it. Ryan was getting worried; clearly these guys had come prepared for a full-scale engagement this time. His ship was an explorer; it was just not designed for combat. The extra firepower notwithstanding, it just did not have the manoeuvrability required.

"Captain on the comm, sir," said Manisha.

"Captain, we are under attack! I am not sure how long we can hold out. They seem to be hell bent on coming for us this time. We're in orbit above your position and will try to draw them away!" Ryan shouted as the ship lurched again to avoid a fourth volley.

"Ryan, your priority is to keep the ship and the crew safe! Get out of here! The tactical situation is in your hands. Do whatever is necessary. Don't worry about us. Leave us here if you need to and come back later!" ordered Anara.

"Understood, but you may not have much of a ship left, if this continues. I'll keep you patched in as long as possible! Ryan out."

"Narada, plot an escape route to the asteroid field. We may need it. Lieutenant, full spread all cannons and two more HEs."

The shots from *Antariksh* exploded near the other ship and it wobbled as the shock-waves hit it. It seemed to hesitate and slowed its approach. Then an answering barrage exploded from the enemy ship, and this time *Antariksh* staggered in space. Power went off and emergency lighting came on.

"Commander, we have been hit! Power distribution throughout the ship has been cut. I need time to set the circuits back," came Madhavan's panicked voice over the comm.

They were sitting ducks. Ryan needed to get the ship out.

"Narada, do we still have steerage and thrusters available?"

"Yes, Commander. We can do limited movement and the projectile cannons are also online."

"Transfer conn back to Manisha. Full thrusters on the course to the asteroid field," Ryan ordered. "Lieutenant, two more HEs spaced apart to give us some cover."

"What about the people on the surface, Commander?" cried out Manisha.

"We'll be back for them. I'm not abandoning our people, come what may. Right now, our priority is to save the ship. Let's get some distance between the ships!"

Antariksh vibrated as all the rocket engines were fired and it started moving towards the asteroid belt. A final volley from the enemy followed but just missed them.

As *Antariksh* gathered speed, all eyes were fixed on the holo to see whether the other ship was following them. It seemed to have stopped on the spot where *Antariksh* had been a short time back.

"I think they just wanted to scare us off, Commander, otherwise why let us go?" commented Manisha breathing heavily.

"You may be right, Manisha, but we can't take that chance - not in the state we are in right now. ETA to the asteroid belt?"

"One hour to the outermost reach, Commander," she answered.

"Find me a big one to land on safely. That will help to carry out outside repairs. Narada, get me a full assessment of the damage sustained and how long it will take to repair. Lieutenant Keisham, keep an eye out for hostile activity. I'll be with Madhavan," said Ryan, getting out of his seat and moving rapidly to the door. He stopped and turned, "I think we've done well, all things considered. Let's see why we cannot come up trumps next time around," he said.

As Ryan walked towards the power plant, Narada came on the comm. "Assessment complete, Commander. Estimated time to repair – forty-eight hours. We will need at least three EVA teams to repair the hull damage."

"Well, I'm sure the Others will find the captain and our team shortly. I just hope they will remain safe till we get back and hopefully the captain will be able to use diplomacy to buy us some time.," Ryan remarked. "These bastards seem to get the better of us every single time!" He was fuming inside – all their preparations and bravado had come to nothing. *Antariksh* had been beaten again, and it was once more running away from a fight, tail between its legs. *Why can't I catch a break?* Ryan thought to himself as he slammed a panel in the corridor.

As he entered the plant, he could see the chaos caused by the firefight. Red warning lights were adorning every display. Madhavan seemed to have restored some power and he could be seen frantically calling out orders to his team.

"You got the assessment, Madhavan?" Ryan asked as he pulled the engineer from the din to a relatively quiet corner.

"I've got it, boss. Narada's estimate of forty-eight hours is valid only if I put every member of my team on the job and pull all non-essential personnel from every other area of the ship," answered Madhavan, wiping sweat from his brow.

"Do whatever you must do. We have a full team down there at the complete mercy of these aliens. We need to get back as soon as possible. Do you have the spares you require?"

"That is not much of a problem, Commander, I have most spares and anything else that is needed can be printed out. The bigger issue is that the hull plating has been damaged here, here and here," he said, pointing out the areas on the display. "We can repair these for a short flight but there is no way we can do FTL speeds."

"Understood, let's get the ship moving first. FTL is still some time off. At least get sub light back on track."

"Yes, Commander."

"We need a new battle plan too. These guys have become bolder than when we met last and I need more tricks up my sleeve when we meet again."

THE KIFRWYSS

ere we go again, thought Anara as she finished her
message to Ryan and raced towards the field
shelter. She needed to warn her people and get
them to safety. The humans of HuZryss could be warned
later; she doubted that they were in any immediate danger.

She was glad to see the full surface team inside the
shelter, except for one security person. Rawat would need
to keep him hidden to be called in when required.

"We have another incoming ship, people! It has already
attacked and possibly disabled *Antariksh.* We should
expect them to land shortly. Let's get the place cleaned up.
I don't want to leave any information lying around for
them. Doctors, get your data encrypted, transmit them to
the pod and shut down your systems. Full lockdown,
immediately!"

"Major, one of your men is not here. You should keep
him out of sight. Listen up everybody, as far as any other
alien is concerned, offer absolute minimum information
and let me do the talking. Is that clear?"

Everyone replied in the affirmative while they
continued cleaning up the systems and securing their
equipment.

Anara went out of the tent and entered the communal
hall. She sought out Joe and Lucy from among the crowd

and pulled them aside. They were surprised to see how agitated she was.

"Listen, we have another ship in orbit and it is attacking my people. Do you have any idea who they might be?"

"Attacking your ship? No, Captain, we have no idea, but it must be the Others. They know where we are located. It was only a matter of time," replied Joe.

"Only a matter of time? But you brought us here. You were the ones who said that we would be safe here. What has happened to that commitment?" she exploded.

"Believe me, Captain. You will be safe here. They will not harm you. We have already sent a message to the Guardians. They will come."

"I am starting to think that your damned Guardians are a figment of your imagination. How come they're never around when needed? They have bloody well left you to rust on this forsaken planet!" she was getting angry at their complacency. However, this was not the time to turn against the only friends she had in this system and she composed herself.

"Tell me something quickly. Do these people also speak English?"

"That is possible but not likely, Captain," answered Lucy.

"Well, then, I need to be able to communicate with them. How will I do that?"

"We will... translate for you."

"Not good enough. I need to know exactly what they are saying. A couple of words can make all the difference in a crisis. Don't you have any translating equipment?"

Anara was not surprised when they said no. Well, they would have to be her translators then. She hoped she would have enough time to open a dialogue and hoped the aliens were not the kind who would shoot first and ask questions later. Her inter-ship communication system was quiet. She'd tried raising Ryan but had not received any response. She desperately hoped that the ship had escaped safely or somehow had managed to disable the enemy vessel. Commander Ryan was good; he would ensure the safety of the crew. She was sure about that. They were running out of time. She needed to do one more thing. The HuZryss needed to know the truth.

"Is there anything else you guys want to share with me about the new people?" she prodded Joe and Lucy. "You must know something."

"We have told you everything we know. We don't know much about the Others, but they were responsible for us having to leave KifrWyss. But they will never hurt us as long as the Guardians are around."

Yeah, but you can't say the same for us, thought Anara. "Listen, I have something important to tell you, but you need to keep to yourselves for now. We have completed the tests. It turns out you are humans after all. Same species as me. You are not the product of genetic modification."

"What does that mean? I don't understand," Joe asked, looking at Lucy blankly. Jim had wandered over and was listening intently over Lucy's shoulder.

"I don't have time to go into the details. Just know that we are all related. There is much more to discover, but for now you cannot share this with anyone - especially not the Others. Promise?"

It was like asking a child to keep a secret. She wasn't sure why she'd told everything to the two of them, but if anything was to happen to the people from Earth, she did not want the discovery to die with them.

"Captain!" the Major called out. "Looks like the Others are here. Their ship is coming in to land."

She sighed and remembered that they were facing a very unpredictable and volatile situation. She needed to resolve this situation quickly and get back to *Antariksh*.

Joe and Lucy led the group out of the hall. It was getting darker outside and they could just make out the shape of the alien ship.

Anara and the Major stood side by side. Whatever preparations they could manage had been done. They now needed to wait and see how the events unfolded. The major fingered the gun on his hip. He was a crack shot but would prefer not to use his weapon. His job would be to protect the team and he hoped that Ryan was up to doing the same job in space. He was now totally focused on one goal only and that was to get everyone safely off the planet. He had two highly trained people with him who would follow every order he gave. One of them would be his secret weapon.

They watched as the ship landed slowly on the pad. The door opened and a few vague shadows stepped out. It was difficult to make out any details, but they noticed that the markings on this ship were the same as those on the ship that had attacked them. At least this time they would be coming face to face with their enemy.

There were five aliens that Anara could make out, who had entered the village. They approached the group near the communal hall, and everyone stopped talking. Rawat saw that the Others were not wearing EVA suits, and that they were carrying a lot of equipment, any of which could be a weapon. He wished his team had also converted their bright EVA suits to darker colours; at least they'd have a better chance of blending in with the crowd. Anara had overruled him. She wanted them to face the enemy with dignity.

Anara adjusted her display and zoomed in on the visitors. The face and body structure of the Others became clear as they came closer. Anara had expected to see human faces again, but what she saw did not shock her as much as she had feared. Instead she was fascinated. This was proof that evolution had worked in different ways on different planets. The Others, she hoped, were representative of the larger population of KifrWyss.

These 'real' aliens were clearly reptilian with vestiges of that nature visible. A cross perhaps between alligators and snakes, she thought. They had thick, smooth-looking greyish-green skin, longish faces and six mismatched limbs. They were walking upright, but she noticed one or two dropping down and crawling on all six limbs, sniffing the ground. The tallest of them would be over six and a half feet. It was impossible for her to tell their gender, if they had any differentiation, that is. What fascinated her were the faces, smooth skin not scaly, snouts instead of noses, sharp teeth when bared, scarlet eyes without lids with an inner vertically closing membrane. They were completely hairless from what Anara could see. The four arms ended in short, hands again smooth skinned. Is their skin smooth all over or do they have scales on their torso? It was impossible to make out below their clothes.

So, evolution had missed the proverbial asteroid hitting their planet, thought Anara, and the reptiles had prevailed in this place. She wondered if the conflict the two species were facing today was a result of their natural aggressiveness, or if it was driven by some other reason. Still she was fascinated by the new arrivals and inwardly hoped that she would be able to resolve the current situation peacefully.

"That, Captain, is an ugly looking bunch," remarked Rawat.

Anara grunted. "Beauty is in the eyes of the beholder, Major. Maybe they are finding us equally unsightly, don't you think? Besides, we should not let appearances turn us into bigots. We have had enough of that back on Earth."

Rawat shrugged. Ugly or not, they looked menacing, especially the one in front, taller than the rest, piercing red eyes blazing away not missing eye contact with the humans. Walking tall, unafraid, literally flexing muscles at every step.

The group reached the communal hall and stopped. The tallest one stepped forward and addressed the humans of HuZryss in a soft, rough tone. Joe and the others responded while the Earth people looked on expectantly, not understanding a single word of the exchange. Joe seemed to be having some difficulty forming words with the hisses and clicks. *Were the hisses part of the language or because of the vocal cords?*

"What the hell is going on?" Anara whispered to Rawat through her intercom. He shook his head, seemingly as perplexed as her.

The alien leader turned toward her as if in response to her whispering and said something. She wished she could understand what he said. For now, she looked at Joe to translate.

"It says – we don't want you here. Go back where you come from," translated Joe.

It? Did Joe just refer to the aliens as 'it'? The alien seemed to realize that the Earth people could not understand what they were saying. It turned around and said something to one of the people behind it, who in turn handed over a few small objects. These were in turn passed on to Anara, who looked at it mystified.

The alien talked to Joe again. Joe then said: "It is a translator. Use it, please."

Anara looked at the small object in her hand, handed over some to her crew and then held her own piece close to her helmet. The alien spoke to her again. This time its voice came clear through her suit. She looked at her team and all of them seemed to be listening to the exchange. It looked like the aliens had managed to isolate the team's intercom frequency and were transmitting on the same. And they seemed to enjoy the advantage of having an English language database. She moved her fingers and adjusted her system to record the exchange and build its own translation database.

"Why have you come here?" she heard the leader ask again, the membrane in its eyes moving rapidly over the red eyes. She could not help staring into the eyes.

She composed herself and replied, "We have come to meet the people who sent a signal to our planet. I think the better question is – why did you call us here and then attack my ship?" She hoped her tone would demonstrate her seriousness. *And by the way – we are pleased to meet you too!* she thought.

Apparently, the aliens understood her well. "The signal was a mistake sent by some of our people who want to expose our world to other species. We are telling you now to go back. We want no contact with your planet."

"And on whose authority are you demanding this? Do you speak on behalf of your government?"

"Government? We do not recognise the Discat's authority in this matter. These new-worlders have been allowed to stay on HuZryss only because of our mercy. We will not allow any other aliens to violate our planets."

"Violate? You call our peaceful intentions a violation? What about all these human lives here on HuZryss?" Rawat felt his temper rising.

"Human life is not our responsibility. We did not call them here; we do not want them here. We removed them from KifrWyss and now we will remove you from HuZryss."

"I don't really care what you have done and what you believe in. I represent Earth here. Since you speak our language and completely lack surprise in finding us here, I think you know more about my planet than we know about yours. I will speak only to the proper representatives of your planet. I will not respond to your threats."

Her own team stood around her equally defiant while the HuZryss inhabitants were listening in shock.

"We have already defeated your ship, you have lost. You have to go back right now, and you will not return." The four 'arms' of the leader thrust forward almost touching her.

"And if we refuse?" She did not flinch.

"If you refuse, then you will stay here forever. You will never see your planet again. Or perhaps we will... kill you today."

Anara thrust her face forward. "That's a very strong threat. I hope you have the means to back that up besides one measly ship." She saw that she had hit her mark, rattling the KifrWyss. They really did not have the power to back up their threats, she realised. Which could mean that while *Antariksh* had not prevailed over the enemy ship, it was still in the fight.

The leader was silent for a while before barking some orders to its people who all pulled out something and pointed towards her team. There was no need to guess that these were weapons.

Rawat moved to draw his own gun, and the leader reacted to the sudden movement, lashing out with its two right hands, knocking out the weapon. Rawat staggered back from the impact, then jumped ahead with a snarl and hit the leader across the torso. The two of them fell on the ground together, hitting and punching each other, throwing up clouds of dust. Rawat was at a disadvantage in his EVA suit, and as the other KifrWyss howled away, egging their leader while the humans recoiled in horror, he was pinned down with four hands squeezing his throat. His security man and Anara jumped into the melee and pulled off the KifrWyss with difficulty. The two adversaries glared at each other, breathing heavily, recognising their equal, their eyes blazing with hate. Anara pulled up Rawat and pushed him behind her. This was not the time to fight. The Earth people were outnumbered. What she needed was to keep these guys talking and learn what she could and give Ryan time to recoup and return.

The KifrWyss pushed her and the crew into the hall. Their weapons were taken away, but their equipment was largely left alone especially the integrated circuits in their suits. She guessed the KifrWyss believed that without a ship, the Earth people were not going anywhere. She was concerned Rawat would fly at the Others again and went to speak and calm him down. The time for escape and for revenge would come.

THE ASTEROID

The dark, naked surface of the asteroid was forbidding but it was a welcome respite, offering the ship temporary refuge from its enemies. The ship lay in the deeper shadow of a high cliff. It sat a little lopsided on the uneven surface, making the task further difficult for the repair crew which moved around slowly in EVA suits. On the other hand, the low gravity eased their burden of lifting the heavy spare parts, providing some relief to the tired crew.

Eighteen hours had passed since the ship had landed on the asteroid for repairs. Ryan had multiple teams working in relays. While he'd ensured all teams got at least a couple of hours of rest and rotation in their work, he and Madhavan had not been able to do the same and he needed all his mental strength to keep focused. They were both at their stations directing their respective teams. Limited power had been restored, but there was a lot more to be accomplished if they wanted to be space-worthy and more importantly battle-ready. Half the ship was still dark and non-essential systems would take many more hours to be restored.

He had been fortunate that there had been no major injuries in the attack. The credit, he decided, must go to the ship's construction as much to the skills of the crew. Or, more likely because the aliens were probably not aiming to kill. That gave him hope that the captain and the team would be safe for a little longer. He had checked all visual and audio records from the ground sent earlier, and they had been continuously monitoring communications from the ground team with zero success. He knew the ground team's data would be uploaded to the pod near the HuZryss's poles and his first task would be to retrieve the logs. He also needed to figure out how to exploit the radio telescope on the ground.

"Manisha, time for Team 3 to return. Prepare Team 1."

"On it, Commander. Ready to go in fifteen minutes. We have completed repairs on areas three, five and seven. Six more to go."

"Copy that. How are we doing on time?"

"Two hours delay on sections two and eight," reported Manisha. "We had two tool breakdowns and we have one engineer injured who's now recovering in medical."

This was going as well as he could hope for. Ryan needed some time to figure out his course of action once the ship was ready. An idea was forming in his mind to get a slight tactical advantage in rescuing his crewmates. It would require a bit of guile and a lot of daring.

***

In the heart of the ship, Madhavan's team was struggling to get power back. The backup generators had been working non-stop for the last eighteen hours and he could depend on them for several days if required. But that would leave the ship low on fuel for backup - especially for the return journey. He needed the main engines back online as soon as possible.

In the back of his mind he was replaying Anara's orders regarding the radio telescope on the surface. He needed to hack into it, but with everything going on he wasn't sure he would have enough time to do that. He had to be near the telescope to scan for its frequency and then find a way to break into the system. He still wasn't sure what the captain hoped to achieve by this whole exercise.

He was also looking for ways to enhance the defensiveness of the ship to withstand future attacks. They couldn't always be running away to carry out repairs. He had thought of increasing the armour on the hull but that would require too much specialised material, which he did not have on hand. There was, however, something he wanted to adapt for defensive use and that was the multi-layered navigation system.

His engineers had identified the exact frequencies of the laser beams being used by the aliens in the two attacks. He thought the aliens would not be able to change the frequency without major changes to the whole emitter setup and it might be possible to build some kind of defensive shield around the ship. He now had two people working on it to match some of his own navigation shield emitters. It had never been tried before, but he hoped it would provide some protection.

Most of the crew had taken to resting in the cafeteria itself, which was churning out endless cups of coffee and plates of food. It resembled a refugee centre with various people curled up asleep in corners and the continuous coming and going of the repair crew. There was some noticeable despair after the latest setback, but many were too tired to think about the enemy or the future. There was just too much to be done, and they didn't have much time.

CAPTIVES

Afew lights tried ineffectually to dispel the growing darkness, but no one seemed inclined to increase the lighting. It was already dark outside, and the warm, dry evening breeze provided some succour from the despair. The communal hall was quite crowded with the crew and humans of HuZryss confined together.

Anara and her team were sitting quietly in one corner. She did not feel like having company right now. She needed time to think and plan the next move. It had been almost twelve hours since their meeting with the KifrWyss. They'd refused to speak to the humans again so far, though she had sent Joe with a request two times. She was disappointed, but not surprised by this development.

They had only slept on and off for a few hours. The suits were not designed for sleeping comfortably and her body ached all over. The doctor was firm that they should keep on wearing their suits. There were organisms in the air that could kill them, and a bit of discomfort was a small price to pay.

She felt the need to move, to get her energy flowing. She stretched and stood up. Three pairs of eyes followed her as she slowly walked among the slumbering bodies. Joe was sitting a few meters away from her and looking anxious. Probably unable to sleep, she thought, despite their body rhythms which were probably adapted to KifrWyss or HuZryss or both. Better get used to this day-night cycle, she might be living the same way shortly, she thought drily.

She gestured to Joe to follow her and they walked together to the corridor next to the hall. It was empty.

"How are you, Captain?" he asked.

"I'm alright, Joe, just couldn't seem to get to sleep. So, I thought maybe you and I could chat and maybe I could find out more about these people who are holding us here."

"Yes. But I have some questions too."

"Why don't you start first then? We have time on our hands – I don't think we are going anywhere soon."

"What is Earth like, Captain Anara? What do people do there?"

Anara smiled at these questions. It was time to tell Joe about Earth. She swiped her forearm and called up a virtual screen. A few commands from her and videos started playing silently on the screen.

"This is my home, Joe," she pointed towards the blue, green and white sphere as it rotated slowly on the screen. "Eight billion people, Joe – just like you and me."

"It is so beautiful," Joe said as he watched the video on the screen, enraptured by the scenes of everyday life. "My planet looks so dull compared to this."

"This is not your true home, Joe. I told you earlier that we are related. Your true home, I believe, is Earth as well. How and why you ended up on HuZryss, I do not know yet. But I promise you that I will find out."

Joe lowered his eyes.

"How about cheering you up a bit? Look here," Anara prompted, "here are our children, Joe," said Anara as images of children playing came up.

Joe raised his head and his eyes lit up. "They are beautiful!"

"Children are how we reproduce, Joe. I guess the KifrWyss are reptilian and may reproduce from eggs and I really do not know if you have seen their young ones. Do you remember your own childhood?"

"Childhood?" he sounded confused.

"When you were younger? On KifrWyss ... in the building?" she prompted.

"Oh, that was long ago. I don't... remember much. We were in... rooms. Many days we stay there. They do many things. It was ... difficult." His voice trailed off.

"I can understand it would not have been easy for people as young as you. How did you get your names?" She had been wondering why all of them had such simple names.

"I don't know. The Guardians said these are our new names. They said it would be easy when people came looking for us."

"Did they tell you who would come looking for you?"

"No. We asked, but they did not tell. We were... taught the new language. But only a few learnt to speak well, but of us learned the language of the KifrWyss."

"Hmm. Okay." She paused, thinking, while Joe kept looking at the videos on the display. She made her decision. It was time to come clean.

"You know, there is something I have to tell you."

He looked sideways at her, inquiringly.

"We found something when we tested you earlier today. One of the women is pregnant."

"Pregnant?" asked a new voice behind Anara.

Anara turned sharply to find Lucy standing there.

"What is 'pregnant'?" asked Lucy.

"Er..." Anara hesitated, embarrassed to be caught in this situation. "It's you. Lucy. You are pregnant."

"What is pregnant? I don't understand," Joe asked.

"It means she is going to have a baby, Joe, a child. The first child to be born on HuZryss. The first true HuZryss."

"Baby? Child?" Lucy seemed shocked.

"Yes. That's … the way humans … multiply … reproduce. The females give birth to babies and then they are called mothers. Lucy, you are going to be a mother! On Earth this is a very happy occasion. And don't worry; I will have Dr Khan explain everything to you. You will of course be telling us all about the father too," she said, smiling and looking meaningfully at Joe. She did not see Jim glowering at them from a few feet away.

She left the two of them whispering to each other and went to find Khan. She needed to brief him and get him to talk to Lucy. And after that she was going to force the hand of the KifrWyss.

As she walked back to her team the door to the hall opened. To her surprise, she saw three KifrWyss enter the hall. She changed her direction and made her way towards them. She stepped right in front of them, blocking their path. Hopefully this would be a positive development.

"Good to see you again," she said, "I hope you've come to apologize and release us so that we can discuss the situation."

"Release? No release. No discussion," said the leader, its voice coming through the translating device. "We have come to see if you are ready to go back. Your ship has returned to pick you up we think."

"I don't think so," replied Anara coldly. "They have not come to pick us up; they are here to send you off." She kept her fingers crossed; hoping Ryan did have something up his sleeve. Time for the showdown. She would not retreat again.

GAME PLAN

*A*ntariksh seemed to be tugging at its reins as its engines reached full power. The superstructure vibrated as the ship came to full life, ready to barrel across space, back on its mission.

The last few hours had been even more hectic on board the ship. Repairs had been completed and with full power restored, the crew had tested all subsystems to make sure they were in working order. Ryan had managed to force two long breaks for the crew in groups and after a few hours of sleep he himself felt more alert and confident.

"The FTL system still needs work but everything else is functional for the moment, boss," reported Madhavan as he stepped into the conference room. Ryan was not sure whether the second in command of the ship should be called boss, but he accepted it only from the engineer.

Ryan waved him to a seat. Manisha and Lt. Keisham were already sitting around the table.

"Lieutenant, you were saying your work on the devices is complete? When can I deploy them?"

"They are ready, sir, but I hope you have considered the implications of what you are proposing."

"Leave that to me, Lieutenant. The responsibility, if something goes wrong, will be mine. Now get me the trigger and prepare for deployment."

The Lieutenant nodded in acknowledgement and left the room.

"May I know what you are planning to do, boss?" asked Madhavan.

"I have a plan, but the risk is too big. It requires two teams to be dropped on the surface to carry out separate tasks." He briefly outlined the plan, causing Madhavan to whistle.

"That's pretty bold, sir. If they don't take the bait…" he stopped talking.

"Then we will be back to square one and probably in a lot more trouble," answered Ryan, flatly. "Now, I have given a list of people to Manisha. They will form the two teams. One danger is that we'll not be able to pick them back immediately once their work is complete, so they need to be prepared for an extended stay on the surface while staying hidden from the aliens."

"Madhavan, I want you to lead one team. Prepare your people to break into the telescope. Take whatever you need. We must break in."

"Sir, aren't you spreading your resources too thin? With the Lieutenant and Madhavan both on the planet we will have no one senior left on board," remarked Manisha.

"You don't think the two of us can handle this, Manisha?" asked Ryan with a smile. She smiled back, a bit more confident but still reserved about her ability to support him alone.

"Anyway, if this works out, we will have all our people safely on board very soon. So, let's go and get this done. Madhavan, remember we need complete radio silence once we're on the ground. We can't risk anyone getting to know you are on the planet. Manisha, it's all on you now. Find a place to land safely near the settlement."

The three of them got up and went into Ops where Madhavan went off to get ready with two people who would be part of his team, one security member and one engineer. The Lieutenant found his team member - an engineer in this case - and the two of them worked out specifics of their plan as they walked off to get ready.

Antariksh lifted off from the asteroid and slowly gained both altitude and speed. Manisha steered it in the direction of HuZryss at cruising velocity while scanning ahead for any ships.

***

"Visible orbit around the planet is clear, Commander. I think they are still on the ground. No indications of other ships from the scans from the pod."

"Keep scanning, Manisha. We don't know if they have someone on the ship looking out for our return."

Manisha moved *Antariksh* in an orbit far from the settlement, and then slowly started losing altitude. The plan was to reach as close to the ground as possible and land several kilometres away. At minimum flying speed using the fewest number of thrusters, hopefully the sound of their arrival would not alert the aliens in the village.

"I have identified a good landing point, Commander," reported Narada. "It is 10.2 kilometres away from the settlement, heading 221."

"Coming about," acknowledged Manisha as she steered the heavy ship with only two thrusters. They were just a couple of hundred meters above the ground - barely making headway. The ship was designed for spaceflight and felt like a deadweight so close to the ground. "Ready to land, Commander," she reported once they reached the designated area.

"Madhavan, Keisham. We're going to land. Be ready and best of luck. Signal when you are ready." They would need at least four hours to make the trek to the site over the terrain in their suits and complete their respective tasks.

The ship landed softly, and Manisha kept the engines idling. The two ground teams opened the airlocks and stepped out. The Lieutenant's team dragged out the anti-gravity transport unit with its heavy device and the five people stepped away from the ship. The ship lifted off, gained altitude and slowly disappeared into the distance.

The ground team turned on the camouflage setting on their suits and, taking turns, they started guiding the heavy anti-gravity unit towards the settlement. There was no ground cover whatsoever. Using night vision, the soldiers led the way, using radars to keep a lookout for the enemy. A few kilometres ahead the two teams silently split up, giving each other a thumbs up; one went towards the telescope and the other moved towards the KifrWyss ship on the pad.

Antariksh reached orbit and circled on the far side of the planet, away from the settlement. It would hide there till the teams on the surface completed their tasks. There was complete radio silence, and the ship would be unaware of what happens on the ground for the next few hours.

***

Madhavan and his two people reached the radio telescope first. Gaining entry inside the structure was easy; there were no fences or guardhouses. The entire area was dark, and their data indicated that they could count on another four hours of darkness. They carefully worked their way through the antennae, resembling those back on Earth, looking for some sort of control room. The engineer saw something in the distance and gestured to his mates to follow. It was a small building without windows. As they walked around it, they found a door in the eastern wall.

The room was completely dark inside. They shut the door quietly and switched on their portable lights. Madhavan was sure there would be some lighting in the room itself, but he did not want to try to locate or switch on the same for fear of setting off any alarms. Either they had been lucky so far or the aliens had not built in any security features, deeming them unnecessary on this planet. He looked around carefully, examining the equipment with its input devices and displays, all dark for the moment, except one which he hoped was the master control.

They set up their own computer in the centre of the room and started work on interfacing with the alien control panels. They believed that they should be able to connect through EM bands. Their system quickly scanned through available channels and identified a potential frequency. Madhavan smiled at the ease with which they had managed to get this done and set to work unlocking the files and finding ways to manipulate them. Lady luck was on their side for once for now.

***

The Lieutenant led his two people through the plains towards the alien ship. The mission was going to be tricky. The absence of light and their own dark visage would help them. They all had IR viewers on in the displays, which projected a very accurate day-like video of the area.

Keisham's display indicated some movement in the darkness ahead. He motioned for the team to stop and crouch. There seemed to be at least one guard near the ships. Keisham moved ahead carefully, using his tactical suit to cover up his heat signature. The guard appeared in his display. There was another heat signature by his side - warm, like a human. But the shape was indistinct.

Ok then, he thought, no uniform or night vision equipment. How did the alien expect to keep guard in the dark night? Something clicked in Keisham's mind. Back on Earth, reptiles can sense heat by picking up infrared radiation. Maybe this guy could do so too. *I wonder how he is keeping warm? He or it?* It was difficult to keep track of the pronouns.

The guard sat down at that point, put down its head and presently Keisham could hear some snoring. He decided to make his move, creeping up carefully till he was a few steps away, then jumping up and at the guard in one smooth moment. He hit the head hard with the butt of his weapon. There was a grunt and Keisham believed the guard had fallen unconscious. He tied up the four brawny arms together, put a tape over the mouth and eyes and covered the face with material from his backpack.

He then examined the strange shape, pushing at it with his feet. The man fell over. "Nish," Keisham whispered. "Oh man, are you hurt?" It was one of the security men they had left back on the planet with Anara.

Nish's eyes went wide on finding his commander standing over him. "No, Lieutenant. I'm all right. They didn't hurt me. Bloody guys caught me just outside the compound. They can see in the dark, you know or sense heat or something. Came right up. I had no chance."

"Ok," said Keisham, lifting the man to his feet. "We have work to do. Follow me."

He motioned the team forward, and they approached quietly looking around for the main entrance of the ship. They located a wide hatch on the bottom, but it was locked with a control pad. The engineer in the team set to work interfacing with the pad but after a few minutes he shook his head and turned to the Lieutenant. "This is not going to work," she reported. Her interface could not resolve the codes.

The Lieutenant nodded and brought out his old-fashioned tools. He could not risk using a laser cutter as it might be visible from the settlement. He slowly set to work opening the various fasteners around the landing gear. They had anticipated that gaining entry might be impossible. Plan B was to set the device in a secure area on the bottom of the ship and hide it as far as possible.

The three of them lifted the device in position and fastened it with clamps and ties. The engineer connected the portable power supply and completed the wiring. She raised her thumb to indicate success, and they closed the fastenings. Then the team withdrew and moved towards the radio telescope to join Madhavan and his group while the Lieutenant sent a single beep to the ship in orbit telling them their work was completed.

***

Madhavan turned around as the second team entered the room. They gave him the sign to indicate their work had been completed successfully. His own efforts had so far not advanced as anticipated. He had quite a bit of information on the language and operating system. Much of this had come from the earlier transmissions from the captain's interactions with the aliens. By using this Narada had compiled some understanding of the language. So far, however, Madhavan had only managed to gain entry to the computer system but finding the correct files in the operating system was proving to be difficult.

After two hours of work, he finally managed to reach the main control section of the computer system. A translation of the controls interface appeared in the display and he projected the same to allow him to use the controls. His work was complete. He sent a single beep to *Antariksh* and the six people settled down to wait – if Ryan needed their help he would get in touch. Till then they had an hour or two to rest and sleep. In the meantime, Keisham took up guard outside the door. It was going to be a long night.

DECEPTION

*A*ntariksh was running at minimal power. The brown planet slowly rotated beneath it. It was day time and the weak sun was shining directly overhead. With their sleep cycles messed up, and tiredness threatening to overwhelm their sense, the crew laboured on. It was only a few hours more. They waited expectantly, scanning around for the enemies and listening for the signal announcing success of the teams down below.

The second beep broke the silence in Ops. Both teams had checked in, their tasks completed successfully. Broad smiles broke out among the crew. The first step had been taken. Now Ryan needed to execute the next phase. He did not want to break radio silence with any of his other teams on the surface just yet. The danger of the aliens intercepting the signals remained, however remote the possibility. First, he had to send a heads-up text person-to-person to Anara so she would know the details of the plan. She, of course, had to contribute to its success. She responded 'Wilco'. Will comply. Dawn was breaking out.

"Right then. Looks like the pieces are in place. Time for action. Open communication to the Captain. Time to play hardball," Ryan ordered.

"Captain, this is Ryan. We're in orbit just above you."

Anara signed with relief – she had been worried that *Antariksh* had suffered a major failure and her people were hurt, but now Ryan was back. She walked to the door and asked for the leader of the KifrWyss. It was easier to call them that than Others.

"My ship is back, and they have a message for you. I am going to answer the commander," she addressed their leader, "and I will do it openly so that you can hear what he has to say. I suggest that you listen carefully." Not that the KifrWyss would have much of a choice, she thought to herself. The text message exchange in her personal display was telling her all she wanted to know. It was encrypted with a person-to-person code so there was little chance of it being intercepted. The leader grunted.

"Good to hear your voice, Commander," she acknowledged while the KifrWyss listened in. There was a movement within the hall as people woke up. Her team was standing behind her and Rawat stepped forward to be right at her side. She noticed his hands were balled up. He was itching for a fight. She reached out and held his hand.

"I hope the KifrWyss can hear me, Captain."

"They can, Ryan. They're right here in front of me," she confirmed. "Putting you on speaker. Go ahead." She looked towards the KifrWyss leader. She couldn't read its expression, if one could call it that, but it was bound to be wondering what was coming next. Its red eyes bored into her, defiant.

"This next message is for the KifrWyss leader," Ryan's voice came back over the translator. "You have kept our people hostage. You have attacked my ship because you did not understand that we have come in peace. In doing so, you have committed acts of war against the people of Earth. I do not know what your motivations are, nor do I care. I only care about my people on the planet below. I will now respond in the same way."

There was silence in the hall. Some, like Joe and Lucy, moved forward to listen closely while the rest stayed rooted to their place. She and Rawat stared back into the eyes of their enemy.

The KifrWyss looked around it, confused as if seeking answers. Then it said: "I don't know how you came back or what new weapons you have, but I am not afraid of you."

"I thought so. So, this is for you."

The humans screamed as a massive explosion shook the ground. Masonry rained on people's heads. The KifrWyss flinched

"That was just a demonstration of my resolve. That was just *one* of the bombs that we are carrying. One of these dropped on you directly would have left nothing but pieces of you lying around. You want more?"

The KifrWyss was not amused, but its ship was on the ground. There was no back up. It had expected *Antariksh* was too badly damaged to fly again. It had made a fatal error and would not be spared. It made a choice.

"You can take your people and go back."

"Unfortunately, that is not going to happen now," replied Ryan. "We will complete our mission and meet the Discat. We are not leaving."

"You will not stay. Our ship just beat you. It will again," said the leader and signalled to its band to get to their ship.

"I would not send anyone anywhere, if I was you," Anara replied. "We have information that you should know."

"That's right, sir. You and your ship are not going anywhere," said Ryan, "so better hand over your weapons."

The leader's nostrils flared. "What have you done?" it snarled.

"Nothing much. It is just that we have your radio telescope under our control and... there is a bigger much more powerful explosive weapon attached to your ship."

"What?"

"A device whose switch is on this ship with me. If you attempt to take your ship or even approach it, I will explode it. That will destroy your ship and the one alongside it. But I realize that it may not be enough for you. So, I have also placed a thermonuclear bomb five hundred kilometres from your location. If that goes off, everything in a hundred-kilometre radius will be completely destroyed. It will shake this planet to its core and cause a winter so deep, nothing will survive. Most likely it will ruin this planet for generations to come. Unfortunately, I cannot give you a demonstration right now, but you can push me if you want and see what happens," said Ryan, flatly.

"Destroy? You will kill your own people... everyone!"

"If I cannot take them with me, then I prefer that we all die here, rather than be your prisoners," Ryan said, hoping he did not sound overly dramatic and these KifrWyss and HuZryss would take his threats at face value. Hopefully, these guys did not know the value people on Earth placed on human lives.

In the control room, Manisha looked at him in shock. He couldn't be serious about this threat. Ryan winked at her and turned back to the screen. "We will be using the radio telescope to send a message to Earth. Our armada is standing by, just one light year from this planet and will be here very soon. I have also programmed the telescope to generate a wide field in this area so you cannot send and receive any signals. So, you see, sir," he emphasised, "you are all alone against me."

Back on the planet, the group of Others looked towards their leader for instructions. It just stood there, seemingly furious and helpless at the same time.

"Call all your people in, now!" Anara ordered. She also saw the messages Ryan was flashing to the rest of the teams, asking them to secure their areas. The remaining KifrWyss loitering around the village had to be rounded up once the 'all clear' sign was given.

The KifrWyss' shoulders sagged in a very human gesture of despair. Rawat moved forward, a smirk on his face and wrenched the weapon from the leader's hands. The KifrWyss were herded into the middle of the room. It was now very crowded in the hall and Anara asked Joe to move some of his people out. A few of them were co-opted into guard duty on the Others.

Anara smiled. Power did flow from the barrel of a gun.

***

"Well done, Ryan! That was a bold move. I'm impressed. So, what do we do now?" asked Anara.

"You got me there," Ryan replied, shrugging his shoulders. He had activated full communications now that the 'Others' were in his control. "This is as far as I could get us. I was hoping the next ace would be up your sleeve!"

"I think we will wait here for some time, Ryan. Let's see if these Others will be a bit more reasonable with the tables turned," said Anara while thinking about her next step. "It will be worthwhile learning more about them, if they are an important part of the KifrWyss political system." She had planned that *Antariksh* and its crew would wait here till the Discat or their representatives showed up, whoever or whatever they may be. But the aggressiveness of the 'Others' was making her fear for the lives of her crew-members and other humans on the planet.

NEW FRIENDS

"Contact, Commander!" called Manisha from her post in Ops. "Third ship with the same configuration approaching the planet!"

"Full alert status, Manisha!" he ordered and red lights came on while sirens sounded across the ship. This was becoming tiresome. This game of new contacts had to end soon, he thought. *How many ships did these KifrWyss have? A new one kept popping up every few days as if following a schedule!* "Let's face these guys. We stop them from landing till we know who they are. Signal the alien ship, Manisha. Tell them not to proceed further. Threaten them if you need to. Let's see if Madhavan's inputs from the radio telescope are accurate."

As soon as Manisha transmitted the signal, the incoming ship stopped in space.

"Incoming visual, Commander," she reported.

"On display, let's see who these guys are. Weapons on standby."

The display resolved into an image of more KifrWyss in their own Ops room.

"You cannot proceed further. This planet is in our control now," Ryan stated simply.

"Your control? We do not understand. Where are our ships?" This exchange in his native language was much easier, thought Ryan. No more playing around with lights and settings.

"We are from the planet Earth. Your ship attacked us, and we had to respond. Your people are now our captives. They have not been harmed but I have a massive nuclear bomb on the planet's surface. Any wrong move from your side and your little planet will cease to exist. This is not a threat but a reality."

"We are not able to talk to our people below. Can you help?"

"There is an EM field that we have set up so that you cannot plan something behind our back. Tell me what your plans are and then we will decide what needs to be done."

"We have come because our human children called us."

"Human children? You mean Joe, Lucy and the other humans?"

"Yes. We left them here so that they could live in peace, but Joe said the 'Others' were coming, so he asked for our help."

"So ... you are the Guardians?" asked Ryan as realization dawned on him.

"Guardians? Yes, they used to call us that," was the reply. "Will you let us speak to Joe?"

"Prove it?"

"Prove what? How?"

"You must have something that proves your connection to the humans below?"

"To prove our connection? Yes, we have something. We are sending now."

A video feed opened on a new display. It showed a group of human children in a facility much like he had heard Joe describe to Anara. They saw the children at various stages of their life up to where they were relocated to HuZryss. Groups of KifrWyss were also visible clearly around the children.

"Narada, facial comparison. Quickly," Ryan ordered. A third screen appeared, displaying the results of the comparison. At least two faces matched the video feed with that of the KifrWyss on the ship.

The video on the display came to an end and a single image flashed. It was a round disc with writing and pictures.

"The golden disk from Voyager!" exclaimed Manisha.

"Yes, it would seem so, Manisha. Narada, visual comparison again."

"The image of the disk is an accurate representation of the original golden record, Commander. I cannot verify when the image was taken, but the image is not of Earth origin," reported Narada.

"Hmm. So, it seems that we have finally met the people who sent the signal to Earth. The theory that someone found Voyager 1 had been proven to be correct."

"Are you part of the Discat?" Ryan asked the KifrWyss on the screen.

"You know about the Discat? Yes. The Discat has sent us. We are the science team from KifrWyss. Are you the leader of Earth?"

"Leader of Earth?" smiled Ryan. "No, I am not the leader from Earth. We are a small crew on this ship from Earth. The ship's leader is down on the planet with the other humans. Her name is Captain Anara. I am her second in command, Commander Ryan."

The KifrWyss seemed to consider this information. "Do you speak for the people from your planet?"

"I guess I do speak for them, yes. We are here in peace in response to your message. There has been too much fighting. This must end now. But till the captain deems it fit, I will keep the nuclear device armed. Do not try to interfere with it or use any weapons."

"We ... assure you. Can we speak to our people now?"

"Thank you. I would like to believe your story and I am sorry we had to meet like this. I'll connect you to my captain and you can talk to your people through my link. How may I address you? Do you have names?"

"I am called RyHiza and I am sorry too. The Others have been disturbing peace on our planet and now it seems they have caused trouble on HuZryss too. I am here to end this trouble."

AN ALLIANCE IS FORMED

"Captain?"

"Yes, Commander. We've heard the exchange. Joe has confirmed the story. He knows the people on the other ship."

"So, what do you say, Captain? Should I patch you through?" asked Ryan.

"Let me think a minute, Ryan. The 'Others' here have also heard what happened and they do not seem pleased with this development. We are having a tough time keeping them in check."

"Do you need more guards?" asked Ryan, suddenly concerned. The group of 'Others' on the surface was considerably larger than their ground party and Anara might not be able to establish control if they started getting violent.

"Yes, I think there is safety in numbers, Ryan. I need you and some facilities on the ship here with me too. There are just too many people floating around here. Do you think you and the third ship could also land here? You can leave Madhavan in charge of *Antariksh*."

"Consider it done, Captain. I'll ask the KifrWyss ship to land, but I will keep them corralled. Then *Antariksh* will land, drop a few people, pick up the major and Madhavan and get back into orbit. We will temporarily disable the three ships down there till we resolve this. At least that way, should more of them turn up, we will have an even chance."

"Sounds good. Anara out."

**

Ryan conveyed the decision to the third ship, and they followed it at a safe distance as it came down to land. *Antariksh* landed a few minutes later and an exchange of people took place as quickly as the EVA's allowed. Fresh EVA suits were also dropped. Ryan and two more people moved towards the hall while *Antariksh* took off and went back into orbit.

We really need a small landing aircraft, thought Madhavan watching the ground fall behind as *Antariksh* rose into space. These multiple landings must be taking a toll on the large ship.

Anara waited for them at the EVA shelter. She was glad finally to be able to change her suit. The strain of the last few days was showing on her and she had tried grooming up as much as their limited resources allowed. She was also seriously tired and desperately needed a hot shower. Only the thought that she would soon be hosting the first ever four-way multi-planet conference kept her going.

"You look beat," remarked Ryan.

"Look who's talking," she retorted, "you don't look so fresh yourself. Still, you are a sight for sore eyes. This has been some adventure!"

"So, what happens now?"

"We talk again and this time we get the final answers." She wolfed down a couple of packs of rations and stood up, asking him to accompany her to the hall where the impromptu conference was to be held.

The sight that greeted them inside was one of hostility, but it seemed to be between the two groups of KifrWyss who stood opposite each other across a rough table in the middle of the hall. They were arguing in low voices. A few of the humans from HuZryss stood around, observing them while Earth security kept a sharp eye on everyone.

Anara opened a comm channel to her ship and confirmed that the major was able to see and hear all that was going on and the proceedings were getting recorded for future analysis. The devices on her team's EVA suits were interconnected to give him a three-dimensional view of the room.

Anara waited for the KifrWyss to finish their discussions. They finally noticed her, and the two groups split up to allow her to come in between. She asked them to sit down while she faced RyHiza.

"I think all the interested parties are here now. Why don't we start from the beginning, RyHiza? You answered the call from my planet and your people have attacked us at every turn. You have damaged our ship and rejected our hand of friendship. On my planet, this would make you our enemy."

She turned to face the other faction. "However, as you have seen by now, we do not give in to threats. We will fight if necessary and we will fight hard."

She stopped, allowing the translators to complete their job and for the message to sink in. "Now, it's up to you to tell your story. Who are these humans on this planet and what do the people of KifrWyss want – peace or war?" she finished rather dramatically.

"This will take some time to explain, Captain Anara," RyHiza answered. It too had red eyes, but they were softer, kinder and while it too stood over six feet tall, the body language did not look threatening. "We know your planet because your people sent a message in a… probe… a long time back. We found it in one of our first expeditions into space and brought it back to our planet. Up to then we had believed ours' was the only inhabited planet in the universe. Like you, we have been looking for signs that life existed on other planets and when the probe was found, we were ecstatic." Its mouth turned into a kind of grimace which Anara interpreted to be a smile, but it was difficult for her to read KifrWyss expressions.

"Our scientists worked hard to understand the symbols. There was a plate that gave good information, but it took us some years before we could hear the voices and then even longer to understand what was being said. We did this in secret and slowly revealed to our people what we learnt. There was much discussion about what to do. Many were fearful because we did not know about you. Were you traders, explorers or conquerors? The Discat decided to wait while we learned more from the probe before deciding what to do."

Another person from RyHiza's group took up the narrative at this point. "The probe was taken to a secret location. We studied everything on the probe and realised that it was from someone who was at least as advanced as we were. It took very long to understand how to read the plate. There were also some sound recordings. Imagine our surprise when we finally deciphered it and understood that the symbols were in... what is that you say?"

"Mathematics," replied Anara automatically. *It had worked! The whole premise of mathematics being the universal language had actually worked!* "And you learned about planet Earth and its people."

"It was not so simple. We could... see and... hear but we did not understand what it all meant. Then came the next breakthrough," said RyHiza, "and we recognized one sound."

"This is like reading a thriller novel," whispered Ryan to Anara. "I almost want to tell him to go to the last page."

"Shh…" Anara whispered back as RyHiza looked at them. They were so close to learning the truth. "Sorry, RyHiza, please continue."

"Yes, the sound. It was what we call h'y'mugh… you call it a heartbeat, I think. A repeating sound – 'bup' 'bup' 'bup'. After that, more words and characters were understood, and we slowly learnt your language. The messages were played for the whole planet as ordered by the Discat, messages of peace as we understood. Still some were not convinced. They said it was a … trick… and Earth people will come to destroy us. Anyway, we kept learning more and more, like your one zero sequence and code. A team was formed to build a translator, and they learned the language. There were some gaps, but the information was very good. That first ship which had found the probe, it had also intercepted some transmissions from your planet. We had not been able to translate those when the ship had returned. But now those transmissions provided us enormous data on your language and culture."

"You betrayed all of KifrWyss, RyHiza!" shouted one of the 'Others'. "Now see what these Earthmen have brought with them - death and destruction. They are not peaceful. They never wanted peace!"

RyHiza looked at them fiercely. "Where is this destruction you are talking about? Don't we have all the ships and everyone on it safe? Are the humans on HuZryss in danger? Is there any destruction on the planet? No! You are the betrayers! You attacked them! You TrueKif are despicable. Attacking our visitors. Attacking these children. Be quiet. I do not want to hear your voice. The Discat will now decide your fate."

"Excuse me," said Anara. "What or who is this Discat you keep talking about, RyHiza?"

"The Discat, Captain, is our seat of leaders for my... continent," RyHiza had calmed down at her question. "We have separate Discats like governments... for all other continents, three in all. They guide and direct our planet. You must understand, we live on one planet, but we have different people in different areas. In the past we lived a simple life and yet there were many... tribes and a lot of fighting. We only recently found some measure of peace. We are hunters by birth, Captain, as I think you now suspect, do you not?"

Anara nodded. Reptiles could be aggressive back on Earth, but she could not extend that logic straightaway to the people of KifrWyss. These people were sentient.

"I believe you found something else on the probe, and the images also resembled some living organisms on your planet," she asked.

"You're right. We have creatures on our planet that look like you humans a little. But we found another surprise. Inside the probe was a hidden chamber."

"Hidden chamber?" repeated Anara. Her briefing and the database had not indicated anything like this. Maybe they had just mistakenly identified one of the components.

"Yes. Hidden deep inside the probe. There we found some containers. They were ... frozen? Very cold. We believe the cold in space kept them ... frozen. These were sent to our science station to be examined."

"And what was in these containers?" prompted Ryan.

"It was life! You must understand we procreate from eggs, but what we found were similar to eggs but ready to hatch. We were surprised and tested them. There was no doubt, this was life."

Anara and Ryan looked at each other. It looked like their database had missed that somehow the scientists behind Voyager had added a secret cargo of human fertilized eggs on the probe. But that did not make any sense. Why would anyone do something like this?

"We did not know what to do. This was more than what our scientists could deal with. The decision was finally left to the Discat. They debated for many days. We had a new life in our hands, but was this the same life you had drawn on the plate on the probe? Our scientists believed so. Then we tested the eggs. I don't know if you are aware that all life requires something, we call K'shaya. Our scientists had always believed that any outlanders we find from other planets would share the K'shaya."

"DNA," said Anara. "We call it DNA. It is strands of proteins that define who we are and what we become."

"Yes, yes K'shaya. Yours was similar to ... animals we call h'jura. Tree living and docile creatures we keep as pets."

"So, you found human eggs, and you found DNA like yours. You know that we also believe the same as you do, that all life is one, but you have proven it before us. We've believed this for generations and it's uncanny that we find the same life source on two planets trillions of kilometres apart." The mystery of life just got a little more complicated for Anara.

"It does seem as you say, Captain, we are all one. Anyway, Discat decided we should try to hatch these eggs. It took us time to determine the correct conditions and method. I am afraid we lost some eggs, but our scientists hatched the rest and those are the ones standing in this room," said RyHiza, pointing to the HuZryss humans.

Anara and her team members had listened to everything they said, and some were crying. It seemed these humans of HuZryss were sons and daughters of people back on Earth.

"That is amazing!" burst out Ryan. "We'd been prepared for many surprises, but this takes the cake!"

HISTORY OF THE HUZRYSS

The three of them sat in the covered entrance of the hall, while the KifrWyss stood in two groups in the sunlight under the watchful eye of security officers.

"So, what do you think of RyHiza's story, Lian?" Anara asked.

Dr Lian shrugged. "It sounds quite probable, but I am not able to understand who put those human zygotes in Voyager and, more importantly, why?"

"The way the thing was described to us, I believe this must have been a part of the design," observed Anara. "Someone decided to send human DNA into space. You know, worst case, even if the probe was not captured by intelligent species, these DNA strands could have potentially landed on a habitable planet and given rise to new life. I realise it may sound far-fetched but..." Her voice trailed off. "I can't help but wonder if this is how we evolved on Earth – someone sent DNA into space and it reached Earth?"

"You have to admire their guts in deciding to allow the zygotes to mature into adult human beings, not even knowing what they would eat or breathe!" said Ryan.

"That's true and we must realise that this whole mission has been based on a number of improbabilities.

The chance of receiving a signal on Earth after we had spent a whole century looking for it, the chance of recognizing the signal, aliens finding a probe in the vast reaches of space, raising human children – it all sounds too good to be true. That being said, this is a scientist's dream!" exclaimed Lian.

"Let's see what else they have to say. Ready to go back?"

***

They went back into the hall. The KifrWyss entered a few minutes later. The four groups took positions around the table in the centre while only RyHiza and Anara were the only one who sat down.

"Everything you've told us so far has been amazing, RyHiza," started Anara. "Tell me, when did you decide to try to contact Earth?"

"You see, Captain, we also realised that this may not be the only probe out there and the originator must be sending other signals as well. We decided to focus our efforts to locate these signals. We set up a team to find those signals. That ... telescope you see on this planet was built by us. My own planet system cannot send signals very far because of the electromagnetic interference in our region of space. We have not had much success with long-range communications." It stopped to collect his thoughts. "You see, we knew about this planet – HuZryss – but this was not suitable for us to live on. The air is dry, it is cooler, and the water is not enough for our needs. Since it was also closer to Earth, we set up a station here and started listening. It took many years, but we found another signal. We understood the message and used the data on the probe and the signals to try to find your planet. We had looked at your solar system many times, but never found any planets suitable to live on, only one large planet mostly composed of gases. We suspected there might be others but could not find any proof."

"So same problem, different solar system," remarked Lian.

"What do you mean?" asked RyHiza.

"It's the same problem we faced back on Earth while looking for planets in far-off solar systems. You cannot see them directly, only postulate their existence based on movements and impacts on the main star. This planet, Proxima B, needed many decades for us to locate and identify as suitable for life. It's just too small. Even now, we believe Alpha Centauri's double star system also has some planets. I was hoping to locate them on this journey, but there wasn't enough time to analyse the data we have collected so far."

"You are talking about our star system, RyK'ya. That is where our home planet, KifrWyss is. We come from two suns and five planets."

"And the increased electromagnetism creating problems for communication would be because of the two suns," concluded Ryan.

"Two inhabited planets in one mission!" exclaimed Lian. "This is unbelievable."

Anara acknowledged Lian's enthusiasm, but there was one more explanation required from RyHiza.

"Why did you send these humans to this planet, RyHiza? It almost looks like an exile to me."

"Exile?" repeated RyHiza, while waiting for a translation. "No, this was for their safety. As we learned more and more about Earth, the opposition to the project also grew. There was a group of people who called themselves TrueKif." It pointed to the group of KifrWyss captives. "They started a violent protest against seeking contact with ... aliens. They attacked the facility where the humans were kept and destroyed it. We then decided to shift the humans to HuZryss to protect them and allow them to live naturally. We were also forced to stop all attempts at communicating with Earth."

"But the TrueKif found them," Anara said.

"Yes, but they did not have a ship to reach and harm them on HuZryss…"

"… until now," Anara finished his sentence.

"… until now," acknowledged RyHiza. "They stole one of our three ships and came here to intercept you. We had already sent one ship to HuZryss. The humans were supposed to meet you and prepare you to meet us. Our last ship brought me here."

Anara was lost in thought as the explanations were done with. She could feel all eyes in the room watching her next move. She had the power in her hand now – the three ships were all in her control. She needed to proceed very carefully.

"What are you proposing we do now, RyHiza?" she asked.

This time RyHiza waited. It had a significant proposal for the Earth people, and it had started to trust Anara. "This is a great moment for the people on my planet. I was sent here to prevent the TrueKif from harming you and to bring you to our home to become part of a bigger civilization."

"Hmm. That is what we have come for, RyHiza. That will indeed be our honour. Just imagine - one small corner of the Universe and two civilizations have thrived so close to each other. But there are still issues we need to resolve. What do we do about the Others who are here now? We cannot leave anyone when we go to KifrWyss."

"The TrueKif will come with us to face trial, Captain. They must face punishment for what they have done. We still do not know who their leaders are, and these people may be able to tell us. I will leave it to you to decide how to do this."

Anara looked at Ryan and motioned for him to follow her. They went to their shelter and connected with the ship.

***

"You heard it all, Major. What do you think?"

"We don't have much choice, Captain. We have limited resources and few options." His vote would be crucial. "I think we should go with RyHiza's suggestion. But rather than of all of us going, only you and I should make that trip. *Antariksh* remains here and keeps an eye on things. We also keep the other two ships in our control and grounded as a guarantee for our safe return."

"We're assuming it is telling the truth about them having only three ships. What if they have more and another is headed towards us full of soldiers?" wondered Ryan.

"It is a chance we have to take. I don't believe they have anything to gain by holding us here or attacking us again? But we will need to be extremely cautious." asked the Major.

"Ryan?"

"I agree. Though I would have loved to see their planet, this is the safest thing to do," he replied simply.

"Captain, you must take me with you!" interjected Lian. "We may never get this opportunity again to see that planet. Even if I cannot take my instruments, I can observe and report."

Anara nodded – Lian was right. "So, it's decided then. We take up his invitation and go. Madhavan, I hope the ship will be ready by the time we get back. It is time to start preparing for our journey back."

"I have completed most of the tasks. We should be as good as new by the time you return."

"Let's get this over with then and return home. And Major, can you see to the disarming of the nuclear devices? I don't want to come back and see the planet blown up by someone tripping over the circuit!"

TWIN SUNS

Anara was completely entranced by the vista that presented itself as they entered the Alpha Centauri system. The emptiness of space was evident once again. She knew there were five planets in the system, but they were not visible to the naked eye. What struck her was the twin suns presenting a majestic view she had never seen before, a larger brighter one and a second less luminous one. From Earth, due to the distance, these two suns often appeared as one.

The journey to KifrWyss had been surprisingly short compared to the months previously spent in space to reach HuZryss. The distance was short and even though the KifrWyss did not have the same FTL technology as *Antariksh*, the ship was quite fast.

The planet of KifrWyss was another wonder, with much bluer than Earth, with deep shades of green and red. It was like a tropical paradise clearly suitable for reptilian life. She could now understand how living on HuZryss could be a problem for these people. HuZryss was practically barren when compared to KifrWyss.

Their ship approached the planet at low speed, giving them a glimpse of cities with low buildings and more waterways than roads. She had never seen anything so peaceful in a long time. It was like an island undisturbed by unsightly concrete and metal structures.

"How come your cities are so simple," she asked RyHiza.

"Simple?"

"I mean, back on Earth, we have mega-cities spread across hundreds of kilometres. The buildings rise many hundred meters into the air."

"Oh. Our… cities… develop under the ground as well as above it," it smiled. "As you may have guessed we require both hot and cold temperatures to survive. The tops of the building are left bare so we can relax during the day and we can go below ground when required. I will show you. All the buildings are connected to a water body."

In the last few days aboard the ship, they had cemented their friendship with the KifrWyss on board. Anara particularly enjoyed the company of RyHiza, the two of them exchanging notes interspersed with discussions about cultures and even philosophy. Their respective translation systems could not always manage to keep up with their discussions, but it had been a deliciously different experience trying to make each other understand the more esoteric concepts of the two worlds. RyHiza seemed to enjoy much more than respect from the KifrWyss aboard the ship, most of them seemed subservient to it. Anara had remarked that RyHiza was probably the most admired scientist she had ever met, even though its field of study remained obscure. RyHiza had remarked that its interest lay across multiple disciplines.

Anara was particularly fascinated with the concept of the Discat peppering RyHiza with numerous questions.

"Captain, your interests in politics rivals those of the best observers on KifrWyss," RyHiza had roared with laughter. "The… government system has… evolved quite late on our planet.   Living in large communities still causes difficulty for some people. Territory and power remain vital pursuits for quite a few." RyHiza stood up. Its cabin was quite small as was the size of the ship. Its head almost touched the low ceiling as it walked to the table and poured cups of steaming hot *manast* for the two of them. Anara took her cup, sipping the delicate super sweet brew. It was a ritual she had come to enjoy, regretting only that she could not share some tea with RyHiza.

"Anyway, we established a hierarchy of the most powerful people on our continent and one of them becomes the leader for life. It is not a perfect system, Captain, but it works."

***

Lian had hit a gold mine when she had determined that there was no gender differentiation among these people. They were hermaphrodites. That surprised her as it was unusual, though not unheard of, back on Earth. She had spent countless hours researching the phenomenon. She had also been provided access to a display port to observe the surrounding space. She had copious notes and date readings and it would take years for the analysis once they returned. Her contact on the ship was quite forthcoming, open, and quite knowledgeable. She was living the dream for a planetary scientist.

***

They donned their EVA suits for the landing, changing the design to ensure prominent gold and blue stripes and displaying their respective national flags. While the ships filtration systems provided safety during the flight, the open environment could be deadly for them. The landing itself was uneventful, as the ship came to a rest on what

Anara presumed was a spaceport. The retinue entered a small building and Anara was astonished to see that it extended ten levels below the surface, right in the middle of a gushing river.

They were escorted into covered crafts which first travelled underwater for some kilometres before ascending out of the water and travelling sedately right in the heart of the city, enabling the residents to get a glimpse of the visitors from outer space. She learnt later that this event had been designed specifically to allow the citizens of KifrWyss see the humans up close and notice their pacifist nature.

The journey to the seat of the Discat made them feel like celebrities. The promenades were crowded on both sides with thousands of citizens watching the procession go by. The two species looked upon each other with wonder, excitement and just a little apprehension. The galaxy would never be the same again. *We are not alone in the universe.*

***

The Seat was a large dark building just a few meters above the water line. It did not look at all imposing, rather Anara found it foreboding, with the dark stone and narrow doorway which might have led to a cave. She wondered if it was all part of an elaborate trap. Rawat too fidgeted at her side. He was carrying his sidearm but what use was one gun against the crowd of thousands. *Have I underestimated the tactical situation and led my team into danger?* But they were committed. There was no going back now.

The party moved inside, walked down a downward sloping roughly carved corridor entered the main sanctum. It was stifling hot inside and their suits took a few moments to adjust to the changed atmosphere before they felt comfortable. The procession stopped on reaching the central atrium with a single seat on a high dais in the centre, surrounded on all slides by water. This was a strange sight for the Earth people who had been expecting a grand palatial interior. Instead it was dark and gloomy, and Anara was shocked to see several delegates lounging around the water as if near a public swimming pool. *This Discat seems quite unpretentious as the most power body on the planet*, she thought. *In fact, they look downright sloppy.*

RyHiza showed them where to sit and it left them with two aides. Anara was amazed to see RyHiza climb the dais and take the highest seat in the house. This guy was the supreme leader on KifrWyss! No wonder everyone else deferred to it and it had done most of the talking. *Just a simple scientist, my foot!*

RyHiza started speaking, its voice resounding in the hall and coming through their translator patch. "First, let me welcome the people from Earth on behalf of the people of KifrWyss. Today our dream has been fulfilled, and we have found friends so close to our planet. We all know the story of their journey and I want to apologise for the hardship caused to them by a misguided few." This was a true politician speaking, thought Anara, not much different from those on Earth. "Like the message from your leaders, we extend our hand in friendship and hope we can work together."

There was a thunderous noise in the hall and an amused Anara realized this was their way of expression. One of the aides nudged her, asking her to stand up, and she bowed slightly, overwhelmed with the welcome.

After the ceremony, RyHiza apologised for keeping its identity hidden from her.

"I needed to do that to understand your people. That would not have been possible if you knew that I was the supreme leader on KifrWyss. I am very happy that we sorted out our differences. Maybe in time we will form an alliance that will suit everyone. The universe is a very big place. We KifrWyss have just taken the first steps. Our ships cannot hope to reach other planets anytime soon. The last journey with the probe was the limit of our capability. There are circumstances beyond my control limiting our reach. But, Anara, that story is for another time."

"I understand, sir," said Anara. "Do forgive me if we treated you too harshly during our first meeting. You are a true statesman, much like our Prime Minister. I wish I knew more people like you."

"We do not know when we'll meet again, Captain, but you will always have a friend here."

"Thank you for everything RyHiza, though I wish we could see your planet without having to wear these suits. I hope you will make a journey to Earth soon."

"That may be difficult, Anara. The TrueKif have been brought for trial, but we have not found the leaders. Their accomplices are creating trouble throughout the continent. I need to tackle this before the Discat will allow me to travel to Earth. But we can still exchange messages and maybe, one day, our wish will come true," he said sadly.

Anara nodded, wondering what the future had in store for them.

THE RETURN

The team used the time on the return trip back to wind down, relax in the hospitality of the KifrWyss and catch up on much needed sleep. They landed back on HuZryss and found *Antariksh* and the other ships just as they had left them on the planet.

There were a lot more smiling human faces this time around. Ryan and Khan greeted Anara when they landed.

"It's good to have you back, Captain!"

Anara smiled back. "I think humanity has made more progress in the last few weeks than in the last several generations. I finally have a pen pal who lives four light years away from me!"

They all laughed quietly, the tensions of the last few days melting away in the pale sunlight.

Joe, Lucy and a few other HuZryss came forward to join them.

"What do you plan to do now, Captain Anara?"

"First, tell me about the baby!" Lucy looked as radiant as a mother-to-be could be.

"Everything is good! The doctor has explained everything to me, and I think I am ready," she said shyly.

"All under control, Captain. I don't foresee any problems and the baby girl will be with us in just a few months' time!"

"I am so relieved to hear that and I'm very happy for you. Your child will be a celebrity back on Earth!"

The HuZryss looked at each other as their smiles vanished. "What do you mean? What will happen to us now?"

"I have thought this over, Joe, and I have asked RyHiza's permission too. I want to offer to take all of you back to Earth with us, if you agree. If, however, you want to stay here, you will be safe. It only asks you to stay on HuZryss till the issues back on KifrWyss are resolved. A few more months at most."

The HuZryss looked relieved at this offer. A look passed through them and Joe reached out to Anara.

"We have been discussing this for the last few days too, Captain. This is the home we know now. We have decided to stay here. Only now, this place will be the first human colony in Alpha Centauri," said Joe.

"We will respect whatever decision you take," replied Anara in acknowledgement.

"But we have one request."

"Anything you want."

"We want our first child to be raised on Earth. In time she can come back to us, but for now let her know the wonders of Earth and we will live through her eyes," Joe explained, his eyes brimming with tears. "Please take Lucy and me with you."

"Of course. We'd be delighted to. We have enough space on the ship, and who knows, maybe we will find your real families somewhere back on Earth. In fact, now that we have your profiles, I am sure we will find traces of your families. I'm sure in time they will come back here to meet you."

"Then, I think, this is as good a time as any to start our journey back. Come Lucy, it is time to leave HuZryss."

***

A few hours later, *Antariksh* was cruising away from Proxima B with two and a quarter more people on board under the care of Dr Khan.

The senior crew was all in Ops preparing their respective functions for the *Jump*.

"Narada, I hope the course is plotted. Are there any other issues that we see, people?"

"No, Captain. All systems go," reported Madhavan. "I will be with the Lieutenant for the first *Jump*, just in case."

"So, this is the end of our first journey," said Anara, settling back in her seat, watching HuZryss on the screen. A human colony four light years from Earth. She looked around at her crew with pride. Most of them had not even been able to see KifrWyss, and yet this was one journey no one would ever forget. Hopefully, they would all come back one day in better circumstances.

"I don't know about all of you, but I am dying to get back home and have a fresh cup of tea."

EPILOGUE

The Chairman's pod landed quietly some distance from the village. A lone figure waiting some distance off walked quickly to the pod as its engines wound down.

The Chairman was the head of the largest and most powerful business house on KifrWyss. Its family wealth went back generations, and the mantle had fallen on its shoulders just a few years back. It had changed the way the family business was conducted – its goal was now power not money alone.

"Tell me what happened?" asked the Chairman.

"Lucy is carrying a baby," answered Jim. "It is how humans breed. She and Joe left on the ship."

"Humph. RyHiza is a fool! It should have not allowed anyone to go back. I made a mistake this time in not destroying their ship. We should have sent a strong message to Earth not to mess with us. That is the way to project power. I now need to gain command to lead our people to greatness!" said the Chairman, in its typical fierce style.

"Yes. I understand. But you will take care of us on HuZryss? You will take us back to KifrWyss?"

"Of course. RyHiza has wronged you by condemning you to stay on this planet. You will be rewarded with a seat on the Discat. The first human on that seat. A human from Earth but dedicated to KifrWyss and personally obligated to me. TrueKif will have power!"

"Now," continued the Chairman, a little calmer now, "did you get the details of the weapon the Earth people had placed on the planet – the thermonuclear device? My people have also built something even more powerful. Perhaps these two will be enough."

"I have it all here," Jim replied as he handed over the data.

"Good! Good! My work is almost complete. It is time for my vengeance. I… will… destroy… Earth!"

Book 2

EARTH TO CENTAURI
Alien Hunt

As Captain Anara and her crew return to Earth aboard their spaceship, *Antariksh*, civil war breaks out in the world they have just left behind. A cryptic message warns her of the dispatch of mercenaries to Earth. Their mission - unknown but deadly. She may have just days to prevent the outbreak of an interstellar war which would bring unimaginable carnage to Earth.

Her crew and the National Investigation Agency engage in the greatest undercover search for the mercenaries in the streets of the megacity. As they race against time to uncover the plot, a traitor is unmasked, and Anara herself comes under suspicion. She must use every ounce of her resourcefulness to protect thirty million people and one unique, innocent life.

Turn to read the first few pages of ALIEN HUNT.

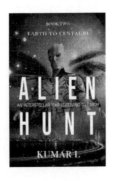

ALIEN HUNT

Prologue

Lucy woke up screaming.

She had another nightmare. The same nightmare. She was still in the middle of this nightmare, if only for a few seconds. It took her a moment to stop thrashing, catch her breath and remind herself that the darkness surrounding her meant she was no longer in that place, even if it did little to make her feel better.

'Lights', she reminded herself. She was supposed to say 'lights'. She whispered it, then a little louder when she realised the AI had not heard her. The room brightened, and she slowly exhaled. The lights didn't eradicate the nightmare, but it made her feel better, if only for a short while. She didn't feel so alone now.

But she reminded herself as she placed her hand on the gentle swell of her stomach, she wasn't alone. Not anymore. Not with the reason she was going to Earth. My daughter will need the love of her people, not the hatred of the TrueKif, she thought.

She lay back on the pillow, trying to get comfortable. She needed the sleep to keep up her strength - Dr Khan had insisted on that. Never having experienced or witnessed childbirth or having had a parent of her own, Lucy had learned to listen and follow carefully whatever the doctor told her to do. In the end, her daughter needed to be born healthy and tough. Anything less would not do for the firstborn of the HuZryss.

***

The Chairman seldom had reason to smile, but it had to admit that the campaign was close to giving it one. Very soon the Discat would be overthrown. Very soon it would rule the land from the West Ocean to the Edge of the East. Very soon the civil war would end in victory. It had taken years of preparations, but the time had finally come to deliver the people of KifrWyss.

And yet it was not happiness, satisfaction or anticipation that filled its heart. No; the burning, acrid desire for revenge saw to that. The Chairman could not abide humiliation, and so the people of Earth would not endure what was about to be unleashed on them. Not vengeance; but justice. Justice for what they had done to HuZryss. Never had the prospect of justice tasted so very delicious.

The mercenaries were ready. The moment was close.

Perhaps, the Chairman supposed, it had enough reason to smile after all.

***

The wounds had opened again. Major Rawat could feel the fresh blood inside his boxing gloves, its horrible wet warmth coating his fists. But he didn't stop. The pain was fuel, fuel for his anger, fuel for each strike against the bag. Maybe, if the pain was terrible enough, it would drive the mission from his thoughts and nightmares. Perhaps he didn't deserve the pain.

Even so. He kept punching.

It was so easy for Captain Anara to make noises about diplomatic victories. As if those hollow words meant a damn thing to those who had spent three days in captivity. As if those words could make up for the sleepless nights and the dreams that came when he did eventually fall asleep. Elite soldiers, his team had been called. It was a cruel joke. Nothing about their conduct had been elite. Calling them herded, helpless cattle would have been too kind. The TrueKif on HuZryss had dominated them, held them hostage and he had been impotent to protect his people.

Never again, Rawat promised himself. With every punch, he said the words to himself. Never again. One more chance to even the score with the TrueKif was all he needed. For that, Rawat would have sold his soul to the devil.

***

Read more. Get your copy of ALIEN HUNT now!

Book 3 – BLACK HOLE: OBLIVION released!

You can sign up for my mailing list for exclusive content and new releases at www.kumarlauthor.com.

Dear Reader,

If you enjoyed this book, please take a few moments to leave a review on Amazon, Goodreads or your favourite site.

Thank you!

Printed in Great Britain
by Amazon